The Outbreak

The Survive Saga, Book 1

Samuel Morris Jr.

This book is dedicated to my wife Christina, my children Samiyah and Sammy, my parents Kimberly and Samuel, and my siblings Daniel, Noelle, and Zuriel.

Chapter One

James Williams was thirty-three when everything in his life changed... again. He was African-American with espresso brown skin and brown eyes. James stood around five feet eight inches tall with a low-cut fade and full facial hair. He worked as a banker, but those skills did him no good during what happened next. His thirteen-year-old son, Robert, had caramel skin and light brown eyes. He was five feet three inches tall with a curly black afro. James and Robert were very close. The events on Christmas Eve 2049 brought them closer.

Their story began as they watched their favorite holiday movie on HoloVision in their seventh-floor apartment. They lived in Morrisville, located east of Downtown Allegheny. Their Middle District neighborhood wasn't as fancy as the Upper District, but it was further advanced than the Lower District. Outside was the worst blizzard since 2010. They both relaxed in their usual sweatsuits. James' sweatsuit was black with a sunset gold Allegheny Gators football team logo while Robert's was green with a skull wearing a Santa hat. He turned to his dad. "What's the craziest thing you've seen?"

James tilted his head and glanced at the ceiling. "Let me think."

He snapped his fingers. "I got it. Four years ago, a scientist illegally cloned a chimpanzee twice. Seeing the three of them together was crazy. What about you?"

Robert smiled. "It's microbots. Have you seen a one thousand microbot swarm form into different shapes?"

James chuckled. "I can't say that I have."

Robert smirked. "You should watch a Holo of it later."

An intense light soared into the air and illuminated the night. James stared out the window.

'*What is that?*' he thought.

It slowed before unleashing a thundering explosion. He rushed to look out the window. In the blizzard, a circular cloud of fire grew in the air south of their residence.

'*What is happening?*' he thought.

The neighboring Morrisville Shopping District was the biggest in the state. It contained hundreds of stores, each with neon on the buildings. A few ran vertical hologram ads into the sky. A tidal wave of darkness swallowed the adjoining neighborhoods. The normal spectacle of the night skyline drowned in blackness as the ring of fire widened. Power went out in their building and the surrounding area. The flames burned brighter against the blackout. Robert joined him. James turned to his son; his eyes filled with panic.

Robert looked at him. "What's happening? Are we under attack again?!"

James opened his mouth for a moment before closing it. He shook his head. "I don't know Robby."

Two more explosions brightened the night sky. One ignited the west, another lit up the east.

He tried to turn on the light on his HoloWatch, but his device was dead. '*Something's wrong,*' he thought.

James turned to Robert. "Bring the flashlights from the kitchen drawer."

Robert ran to grab them, but they wouldn't power on.

A woman pounded on the door. "Help me!"

James and Robert jumped.

She banged her fists again. "Please! Open the door!"

Robert followed James past the couch. With no electricity, James pulled the manual release to crack the sealed elevator style doors. Robert yanked them apart, and the woman scrambled into the residence.

She forced them together and whispered. "Lock it."

James pushed up the lever. He pivoted to the stranger to ask what was happening, but she placed a finger to her lips. She was James' height with blonde hair, blue eyes, and ivory skin. The stranger wore a mustard yellow peacoat. Then he heard a noise unlike anything he'd ever experienced. It sounded like a lion's roar with quick pulsing intervals, but something was weird about it. The weirdness shot shivers down his spine.

'What was that?' he thought.

The sound emanated from the corridor. Something banged against the door. They jumped back. His heart throbbed. Another impact dented them in the middle. One more blow split the top of the doors apart. She grabbed their hands and dragged them to the right down their apartment hallway. They passed Robert's room on the left, the bathroom on the right, and entered the master bedroom straight ahead.

James and Robert scrambled under his king size bed while she closed the folding closet door. The front doors took one last hit, and they heard another pulsing roar. Whatever broke through was now inside their home.

James felt the power of its steps as it strode. The pulse roars grew louder as the creature got closer. He turned to Robert and held his finger to his lips. The creature entered the room and paused. Its feet had small claws on them, but its skin brightened the entire area as it blazed neon sign blue.

The creature roared. It went to the left wall window. The creature lingered there before turning. It let out one more roar. The woman opened the closet and ran towards the front door. The creature pulse roared at a high pitch. James and Robert covered their ears. It leaped over James' bed and pursued her. The stomping grew further away. James heard a thud and a roar. A haunting shriek of suffering followed, and then silence.

He exited from their hiding spot.

Robert grabbed him. "What're you doing?"

James glanced at him. "I'm seeing what's happening."

He planted his back against the wall near his bedroom door. James peeked into his hallway for any trace of the creature. The hall was empty. He waved Robert out. His son accompanied him. They investigated Robert's room and the bathroom. As they moved to the living room, James gawked at their bent front doors. Both sides now curled into the dwelling. The main hall was lit by the creature's blue glow. They put on their boots. James poked his head out into the corridor. The neon blue radiance of the creature's flesh emitted from his left. Its muscular back was to him. It kneeled with the stranger's neck in its jaws. He observed her veins darken under the illumination of its body.

She laid on the ground just before the GravLift. The hue of her killer illuminated her face as her dying blue eyes stared into his. Robert peered into the hallway. James covered his mouth to stop him from screaming. Their neighbor from across the hall exited his apartment wearing a bathrobe. He was on the heavier side, bald with beige skin.

The man rubbed his eyes and squinted at them. "What's happening?"

James and Robert motioned for him to be silent and pointed at the creature. The man fell onto the hall floor. It loosened its grasp and turned to him. They dodged back into their residence and hid behind the bent doors. James studied it through a crack. The creature was a physical specimen, with the muscles of a bodybuilder. He saw its jaw through the decaying cheeks. Its razor-sharp teeth had crimson and navy dripping off them. The creature's eyes were black as space. Blood dripped from its clawed hands.

'*What the hell is that thing*?' he thought.

The neighbor screamed and raced right towards the east stairs. The creature pulse roared at a high pitch and charged past their residence. They poked their heads into the corridor after it passed. He banged his shoulder into the stairwell door, but it wouldn't open. The creature captured him. It sank its claws into his shoulders and swung him into the metal doors of the apartment at the end of the hall. The force dented them. The creature kneeled over the man and clasped its jaws around his neck.

James pulled Robert left toward the center stairwell. As they approached the stairs, he glanced at the stranger. The fire from the explosions illuminated her through the GravLift's glass walls. James and Robert avoided her body, trying not to alert the creature.

As they entered the staircase, more neighbors moved into the hallway to investigate the blackout and the commotion. Once they saw the creature, people screamed and forced their doors shut. Some froze in terror. It dropped their neighbor's neck and turned. The creature jerked its head in every direction as it pulse roared in a high pitch. Its attention held on a door to its immediate left that was closing. The creature threw itself into the door shoulder first until it broke.

Two more creatures arrived from the west stairs on their right. A man and two women who'd froze at the sight of them dashed towards James and Robert. A creature seized the man as he fled. The other gave chase to the women.

They ran into the central staircase, followed by the women and the creature. One was a redhead with porcelain skin, while the other had blue hair with purple highlights and warm ivory skin.

As the four of them descended the glass walled stairwell to the sixth floor, the creature rushed in behind them. When James and Robert passed the fifth floor, another monster burst out and grabbed the redhead by her hair. It chomped her neck as her blue-haired girlfriend stopped and screamed. Her tattooed right hand covered her mouth.

James saw the creature that followed them down the steps nearing. "Look out!"

The woman with blue hair and purple highlights wasn't strong enough to fight the creature. It forced her to the ground next to her girlfriend and locked onto her throat. She grabbed her girlfriend's left hand with her right. Each hand had the same half broken heart tattoo.

James pulled Robert. '*We have to get out of here now.*' he thought.

As they rushed down the stairs from the fifth floor, yelling erupted from every direction. A vast pool of blood covered the landing on the fourth floor. They peeked at the square window on the door. A bloody handprint stained the inside of the glass.

As they descended from the third floor, someone dashed in on the ground floor. A creature banged through the door before it closed. He ran halfway up the stairs before it pounced on him.

They exited the stairwell on the second floor. The first levels had glass doors. This part of the corridor was open on one side and overlooked the foyer. The facade of the building featured a two-story windowed entryway. As they raced right towards the west exit, they saw people running into the lobby, away from more of the creatures that neared the shattered glass front doors. Other victims' necks were inside powerful jaws outside the entrance. The air was thick with the smell of blood.

As they reached the staircase, James froze. '*Oh no.*' he thought.

A creature turned to face them, and pulse roared. They dared not move. Its head twitched in sudden motions, almost inquisitively. Then it moved down the steps toward the ground floor. They both panted.

Robert gazed up at him. "Why didn't it attack us?"

James peered at him. "I'm not sure."

They pressed open the first door and crept outside through the second. The icy wind howled. The chill bit at their faces and hands. Several inches of snow accumulated on the grass and shrubbery surrounding the apartment. Less accumulation was on the heated roads, but they still looked precarious. Robert was starting past his father, but James pulled him behind a bush to their left. He pointed at the street where a brunette woman laid. A creature latched onto her neck while facing away from them.

He leaned in and whispered. "Keep alert."

Robert glanced around for any other creatures. As James continued scanning the area, he spotted Sofia Hernandez from the sixth floor. She was a twenty-nine-year-old Colombian with light tan skin and brown eyes. Sofia was five feet one inch tall with black hair past her shoulders, full lips, and a beauty mark below her left nostril. She wore blue jeans, a black winter coat, and matching boots with fur. Sofia kneeled in the snow, shaking behind the shrubbery to their right.

He started towards her. Robert gripped him and whispered. "What're you doing, dad?"

James pointed to Sofia. "Going to help her. Stay here."

Robert shook his head. "What if that happens to me?"

James stared at the creature's back as it dined on its victim. "I'm pretty sure they can't see us if we don't move in front of them. I'll be right back."

He turned and Robert dragged him backwards. "You don't know that."

James exhaled. "No, but think about it. That creature looked straight at us and didn't attack when we stayed still. They attacked the people who yelled and ran."

Robert's brow furrowed.

James grabbed his son's shoulder. "Don't move and stay quiet. I need to help Sofia, and then we'll go to the HoverCar. Wait here."

Robert exhaled and nodded. James crept to her on the snowy grass. '*I hope the wind is loud enough to cover my steps.*' he thought.

After the tense fifteen step journey, he reached her. Sofia shook, blind to his presence as she stared at the victim. He waved his palm in front of her face, then clutched Sofia's mouth to prevent her from shrieking. Her widened eyes looked sideways at him. He whispered. "It's me, James. I'll get you out of here. Be silent and move slow, okay?"

She acknowledged and gripped his hand. He monitored the creature. It freed the woman's neck and rose. The creature spun toward the building.

James ducked behind the bush. '*What do I do now*?' he thought.

Broken glass rained from the second floor. A man jumped through the window and landed between them and the creature. He cried out in pain.

The man pounded the ground with his fists. "My legs!"

The creature advanced towards him and let out a pulsing roar. He peeked up and struggled to crawl away. It jerked its head around before pulse roaring at a high pitch. The creature focused on the crawling man. It leaped on him and dug its claws into his shoulders. He shrieked in agony.

The man shouted. "Someone, anyone... help." The creature bit his neck, and his body went limp.

Sofia buried her face in James' chest. A baseball sized rock flew past the creature's head. It dropped the man's throat, turned, and roared. Another stone shot further down the road. It chased that one. The creature released a high-pitched roar.

James scanned the area. Robert held a large rock. He motioned for them to come after he threw it. James nodded. Robert tossed it further down the street surrounding the building. The creature tracked it and roared again. They moved to him.

James patted him on the side of his shoulder. "Quick thinking. Thank you."

Robert shook. "I had to stop you from dying."

Sofia leaned over and kissed Robert on the cheek. "Thanks."

He stopped shaking and blushed.

She gazed at the fallen woman. "Can we leave, please?"

James nodded. Sofia grabbed his hand while Robert was on his other side. As they went towards the front parking lot, they came to a halt. He studied the steel parking stations. Creatures were everywhere.

Robert peered at his dad. "What're we going to do now?"

James turned to Sofia. "There's a ton of them by my HoverCar. Do you have one?"

She shook her head. "I use the Shofer app to get to work."

He stared back at the infested parking lot. "I have to reach mine."

She gawked at him. "You'll just get yourself killed."

Robert nodded. "She's right."

James scanned the vicinity. The community pool and lifeguard station were across the road. Further up on the left was a smaller two-story apartment building. Its parking area was full of creatures. A hill at the end of the drive led to the primary street.

He looked at them. "Here are our options. We go for the car with these creatures everywhere. We make a break for the main road on foot past more of them or we stand here and freeze to death. Getting the HoverCar is the best choice."

Robert and Sofia stared at the vehicle with worry in their eyes. When he took his first step, he noticed movement in the darkness. A man was running towards a red car. The creatures near the parking stations pulse roared in a higher pitch as he ran between them. He entered his HoverCar, slammed the door and tried starting the engine. A swarm of them engulfed the automobile. They pounded through the windshield and windows. The sounds of cracking glass and the driver's screams replaced that of the struggling motor. The screaming stopped after a moment.

Sofia trembled. "What now?"

He peered at multiple cars with their doors lifted. They were empty. "The HoverCars might not work. The explosions must have fried their operating systems and the power grid."

He studied the parking lot across from the adjacent building. "So, the car was a horrible idea."

They both nodded.

He exhaled. "Okay, we'll move around the pool house, then use the HoverCar stations as cover to reach the complex entrance. Then we head uphill to find help or safety."

Sofia nodded. "Let's go."

They moved behind the brown brick pool house to the first station and stopped. James peered in between it and the next one. The coast was clear. They advanced between stations until reaching the last. *'We're almost at the hill.'* he thought.

He peeked past it. There stood a creature turning in their direction. He held up his palm and froze.

James stared into the black abyss of its eyes as it looked above him. *'Does it not see me? Does it not smell or sense me either?'* he thought.

The moment lingered in the air, as he dared not flinch. Then they heard barking from uphill. A Chocolate Labrador with a sunset gold collar ran down the hill. Monsters pulse roared at a higher pitch as they rushed after it. The creature turned and roared as it moved to join the horde. Other creatures in the proximity followed.

He put his back against the HoverCar and hyperventilated. *'That would've been bad.'* he thought.

James slowed his breathing and glanced around the edge of the parking station again. Once the last creature left the vicinity, they proceeded to the hill. He peered down the slope as the monsters followed the dog. The breeze stopped as big, wet snowflakes fell. James cupped his hands in front of his mouth. He attempted to heat them with his breath, to no avail. They still hurt from the chill. He placed them into his hoodie's pouch. James watched Robert, trying to warm up as well. They heard faint screams of fright and suffering from other apartment complexes downhill. He studied the two-story brown brick buildings. The howling wind replaced the howls of pain. They looked at James.

He shook his head. "Let's get going."

They nodded and started uphill. James followed them.

He glanced back as he strode. *'I must protect them. We've got to find help.'* he thought.

James moved ahead of them. They walked up the sidewalk, struggling not to slip and slide backwards in the inches of wet snow. As they struggled to the hilltop, they noticed more creatures wandering around the shopping plaza. In the moonlight, they saw hundreds of them. Wrecked HoverCars blocked the road with open doors and blood on the concrete near them. The Charge 'N Gas station was down a small hill close to the entrance. As James gazed at it, he noticed a vehicle crashed into one of the gas pumps. Smoke billowed from its hood as gasoline poured out from the dislodged pump. The car caught fire. He gripped their hands and pulled them faster.

As they got to the intersection, the fuel exploded with earth shaking force, knocking them to the ground.

They stood and watched the flames and smoke shoot into the air. All the monsters in the parking area moved towards the explosion. They looked downhill at the shopping district and saw creatures moving uphill. On their left, they noticed blue glows approaching from the police station's direction. The lights were creatures and not the salvation they hoped. They glanced at their apartment complex as monsters emerged from both buildings. The creatures advanced to the source of the shaking. All three groups closed in on them.

They watched the creatures in the plaza gather around the fire. Their skin looked red and yellow in the radiance of the flames. They listened, but there were no sirens. No help was coming. They had nowhere to go and nobody to save them.

Sofia stared at James. "What do we do now?"

He surveyed the scene. "I don't know."

Chapter Two

As the creatures headed their way from three directions, James surveyed their surroundings. *'How do we survive this?'* he thought. Robert put his hands on his head.

He turned around, hit his dad on the arm, and pointed. "Look!"

James turned and saw headlights of a classic S.U.V. moving towards them. The all-black vehicle sped up the hill through the falling snow with monsters pursuing it. The creatures coming uphill from the apartments focused on the truck. James, Robert, and Sofia waved their hands. The driver swerved past the horde and slid to a halt in front of them. "Get in!"

A dog barked in the backseat. They entered as the monsters near the gas station approached. Creatures slipped on the snow while in pursuit. The tires spun in the slush before catching their grip. Multiple creatures pounced at the S.U.V. One latched onto the trunk. As they drove downhill toward the shopping district, they swerved through the monsters on their way uphill to the explosion. The creature climbed to the top of the truck. Sofia and Robert ducked in the back seat as it pounded. The dog yapped upward.

James dropped. "It's on the roof!"

The driver stared at him. "First rule of survival."

He took a hard right and drifted on the main road sideways.

The monster flew off the vehicle as they slid around the corner. "Stay calm under pressure."

James looked closer at him. He had beige skin with brown hair, full facial hair, and blue eyes. The man wore a black police uniform with sunset gold accents.

The driver extended his hand. "Officer Liam Smith. Who do I have the pleasure of saving tonight?"

He grasped it. "I'm James Williams, that's my son Robert, and that's Sofia Hernandez."

Liam glanced at the rearview. "Nice to meet you."

She leaned forward. "Thank you for stopping. I'm not sure what we would've done if you hadn't."

Robert smiled. "Yeah, thanks. We had no options when you stopped."

Liam nodded. "My father says 'Our work is aid. Take pride in your work.' When people are in need, it's my duty to serve."

She struggled to smile at him through her jitters.

Sofia turned to James. "Thank you for saving me. I'd be dead if not for you."

He turned to her. "No problem. I couldn't leave you there."

She exhaled and sat back.

Liam pulled the S.U.V. over past the shopping district. "We're clear for a second. Let's make a plan."

Liam turned towards James. "My dad has been an officer for ninety-five years. I know he can handle himself. I wanna check in with him at the station just to be sure. We'll be safe there and seeing my dad will put my mind to rest. There's one more seat in the truck. We can pick up someone important to either of you." James peered at Sofia.

She grabbed her locket. "My parents died in the bombing on the North Side last year. So, there's nobody for me to save."

James took her hand. "I'm so sorry for your loss."

She nodded at him.

James glanced at Robert. "His mother is the person for us."

Robert turned to the window.

James stared at the dog. It had a sunset gold collar. "Is this your dog?"

Liam shook his head. "Nope. A group of those creatures were chasing him. I couldn't just leave him there."

James rubbed the Chocolate Labrador's head. "He saved our lives."

Liam smiled. "Well, isn't this a truck full of heroes?"

Liam shifted the S.U.V. into drive. As Liam sped towards the on ramp, he passed under a red sign that read Merry Christmas in green lights.

Liam chuckled. "Merry my ass."

The highway was a desert of slush. Heated roads only melted half the snow in heavy precipitation. Not ideal conditions for classic car owners. Their cars still used tires, while HoverCars controlled the same in any weather. The meteorologist advised people to stay indoors. Most folks heeded the warning, except for the last-minute shoppers.

As the vehicle powered through the elements, James turned to Liam. "What the hell is happening?"

Liam peeked at James. "Your guess is as good as mine. One minute I'm talking with my old man and the next there're explosions in the distance. My HoloWatch died, and these creatures appeared out of nowhere. Then I discovered the dog, and you lovely people."

James gazed at the passing scenery. "The east side of the city lost power. No HoverCars are working. How's this thing running? No offense."

Liam shot James a look. "Much taken. This 'thing' is a classic that saved your ass."

James put up his hand. "True enough. I apologize."

Liam shook his head. "Don't apologize to me, say it to Terri."

James scratched his skull. "Who is Terri?"

Liam scoffed. "You're sitting in her."

James chuckled. "Sorry Terri."

Liam grinned. "She forgives you."

James glanced in the mirror at Robert and Sofia. They were both staring out their windows. The dog's head was in Robert's lap.

James turned back to Liam. "Thank you again for stopping. We appreciate it. I'm not sure what we would've done if you hadn't."

Liam tipped his imaginary hat towards James. "Just doing my duty. I was outside the city when the explosions occurred. Plus, this baby isn't reliant on operating systems and 6G networks for auto piloting like HoverCars. This was my grandfather's truck. He gave it to my father, and my old man gave it to me. A classic from when you steered the car yourself. Way back in 2019."

James nodded. "You don't see many of them anymore."

Liam smirked. "Call me exceptional. Just don't call me a hippie. You'll have to walk if you do."

James snickered. "Were you able to help anyone else?"

Liam shook his head. "No. I was going home through the business district. With the power out, the neighborhood was a winter ghost town. The blackout cut my conversation with my dad short. I wanted to call him back and finish it, but my HoloWatch didn't turn on after the explosions. At a stop sign, I noticed a creature headed right for me at the last second. It came out of nowhere and jumped onto my hood. I slid into an intersection, and the creature lost its grip. Sound familiar?"

Liam cleared his throat. "I turned the next corner and swerved between dozens of these creatures. They followed me. As I drove into the residential district, a woman laid in the snow with a creature clamped on her neck. It released her and pursued me too. They can't move in this weather. As I came up the road where I met you, I looked at the apartment complexes. Seeing them overrun, I'll never forget that... or that woman."

James peeped at his son in the mirror and then concentrated on the pavement. "Several people died in front of us. A number more were dead. Others hid and ran for their lives. We heard their screams as we fled and then... nothing."

James paused for a moment. "I'm uncertain if anyone else escaped our building alive. There are one hundred eighty apartments in that tower."

James clinched his fist. "I hope more people got out, but my only priority was Robert's safety. When I saw Sofia there, I had to help her."

He looked in the rearview and caught her smiling as she stared out the window.

James closed his eyes. "I tried to save the woman that banged on our door. When the monster entered the room, we hid in my bedroom. She panicked and tried to outrun it."

'Who was she?' he thought.

James shook his head. "If we attempted to save that other woman and her girlfriend, there's a chance we'd be dead. If we died, maybe Sofia wouldn't have survived."

Liam put his hand on James' shoulder. "You can't focus on what you weren't able to do. It'll drive you crazy. I knew an officer who shot a criminal that was robbing a store. He walked in, the guy turned towards him holding a gun. You don't have time to think. Reaction speed is your best skill at that moment. The owner, the community, and his fellow officers called his act heroic. He saved that woman's life. The next day, he resigned."

James raised an eyebrow. "Why did he resign?"

Liam looked at James. "He didn't feel like a hero, or someone we should celebrate. Would the suspect have hurt the owner? He believed he should've deescalated the situation. I don't agree with him, but I understand his point. That reaffirmed to me that if we stay in the past, we won't move forward. History is full of regrets. You must live for this moment. Right now, we can use that mindset."

James nodded. "You're right."

Robert leaned between the front seats and looked at Liam. "Can't this truck go any faster?"

James glared at him. "Sit back."

Robert slammed into the seat as he sighed and crossed his arms.

Liam stared in the mirror. "Hey, respect the classic. It's bad enough there're dents on my hood and roof. I'd prefer no damage inside."

James scowled at Robert.

Robert unfolded his arms. "Sorry Liam. I just want to save my mom."

Liam nodded. "We're driving through accumulating snow and slush on a dark highway with tall drops on either side. Even with expensive new tires, one slight mistake in this weather and we'll never make it to your mother. This isn't a HoverCar."

Liam sighed. "I realize you're scared and you wanna reach her. Feeling the same way up here. I'm worried about my dad too. Being safe is more important than speed. We must take care of us first to reach the ones we love. They'll be with us soon."

Robert didn't respond. He continued staring out the window. Liam shook his head.

James leaned over. "I apologize for his behavior."

Liam waved it off. "It's not a big deal. I understand how he feels. He's not the only one freaking out about a parent."

James smirked. "I thought the first rule was to stay calm under pressure."

Liam rolled his eyes. "Do as I say, not as I do. Besides, I'm tranquil on the exterior. People can't see inside. I've closed the blinds."

James took notes on an imaginary notepad. "Got it."

They both chuckled.

James cleared his throat. "I'm sure your dad is okay, but I would've understood if you saved him first. Hell, you didn't have to pick us up, but you did."

Liam nodded. James turned and observed Sofia as she bit her nails.

He touched her knee. "How are you doing?"

She shook her head. "Not great. This entire day was a roller coaster."

James studied her eyes. "What else happened today?"

She chuckled. "I quit my job."

"Was that good or bad?"

"It was overdue. I was a store manager for an inappropriate jerk for a year."

James frowned. "Inappropriate in what way? If you don't mind me asking."

She smiled. "Not at all. He assumed I wanted him because he made good money. I set him straight a few months ago. That only caused him to pursue me more. Every time I said no, he tried harder to win me."

James rolled his eyes. "Oh, he's that type of guy."

She sighed. "I was searching for a new job. Today was the last straw. He grabbed my ass as I walked by him."

James stared at her. "What did you do?"

"I told him I had enough of the harassment and that he'd be hearing from my lawyer. When I stepped towards the door, he called me an ungrateful bitch. I turned and punched him unconscious."

James laughed. "You knocked him out?"

She smirked. "Either his jaw was glass, or I'm a superhero. I knocked him out and left."

Her smile faded. "When I got home, I called my friend Lydia. While I sat on my couch, I decided to concentrate on my goal of being an entrepreneur. I can't accept being an employee anymore. Working for him showed me how to not be as an employer. Lydia stayed on the second floor of our building. We planned to celebrate me quitting. She wanted to change out of her uniform at her apartment first. Lydia worked at the grocery store by the Charge 'N Gas station, so she'd walk there. Between the approaching storm and her job not being busy, they sent everyone home early with pay as a Christmas gift."

Her eyes watered. "Lydia was dead in front of me when you arrived."

James grabbed her hand. "I'm very sorry that you had to witness that. Tell me if you need anything."

She put her other palm on top of his and tried to smile. "Thank you James. You've already done a lot for me tonight."

He turned to Robert. His brow furrowed as he stared out the window.

James tapped his knee. "We're moving as quick as we can. I recognize you're worried; I am too. Look at me."

Robert looked at his father

James peered at him. "We'll get your mother."

Robert glanced down. "I'm scared. What if something happens to mom?"

James shook his head. "Don't speak that into existence. We will do everything possible to prevent that. Positive thoughts only."

Robert nodded. "Okay dad. I just want her to be safe."

James smiled. "I know buddy. We're almost there."

Robert stared back out the window. James faced forward.

Liam squinted at him. "You should fasten your seatbelt and face forward. This isn't the weather to play crash roulette."

James saluted Liam. "Sir, yes sir." He secured it. "Mission accomplished, sir. Anything else, sir?"

Liam smiled. "We have another wiseass in the car. There's only room for one in this vehicle, so I guess we battle. Loser has to leave."

James grinned. "Comedy is how I stay stress free. I focus on smiling and laughter for others and myself. It helps me get through my days without popping multiple gray hairs."

Liam nodded. "I understand that. Good jokes make life better. Please, continue to call me sir."

James laughed "Yeah, okay Liam."

Liam turned to him. "I was serious. It made me feel powerful and respectable. I liked it. From now on, my name is Sir Liam Smith."

James laughed. "You can't knight yourself."

Liam glanced back at him incredulous "Number A, I'm not claiming to be a knight. Letter two; I can do what I want. This is America."

They exited the deserted highway and drove through Leo Creek. It differed from Morrisville. As a Lower District neighborhood, the neon and advancements of the last thirty years barely touched it. Except Ariel's Coffee. It was everywhere in the world. The contrast was jarring each time James picked Robert up from Candace's apartment. It put things into perspective and made him appreciate the home he provided his son.

James saw Liam tapping his fingers. "Thinking about your dad?"

Liam nodded. "A little. I'm sure he's fine."

"What were you and your dad discussing?"

Liam cleared his throat. "My father is the Captain of my precinct. His bones are turning to dust, and he's been contemplating retirement, so he'll need to be replaced."

Liam turned to James. "He nominated me to be his replacement earlier today."

James saw Liam's eyes widen. "That's a good thing, right?"

Liam shrugged. "Yes. Or at least it should be. Other Lieutenants were there longer than me. They're more qualified based on tenure alone. I'm not viewed by some as serious enough. Can you believe those stinky heads?"

James and Liam chuckled.

The smile faded from Liam's face. "I'm a hell of a cop. Top of my class and I take my duty seriously. How am I supposed to lead people with more experience than me?"

James smiled at Liam. "With grace. They may have more experience than you, but your old man nominated you. He sees something in you. Ask him what later. They might offer you the position, or they extend it to someone else. See how it plays out."

Liam cleared his throat. "They offered me the role immediately after his nomination."

James grinned at him. "What are you going to do?"

Liam's brows furrowed. "I'm not sure. What if I'm the wrong choice?"

James grabbed his shoulder. "If your dad and his superiors think you're perfect for the position, why don't you?"

Liam shrugged. "I've never led anybody. What if something terrible happens under my watch?"

James removed his hand. "That's a valid fear, but they offered it to you for a reason. You must be awesome to be a lieutenant already. You saved us. That makes you heroic. You may not be a good leader yet, but you can learn. Your father might demand greatness from you because he sees it within you. Don't live in your fears."

Liam beamed at James. "You're right. When we get through this, I'm taking the offer. Thank you for the advice. You helped me look at this from another angle."

James nodded. "No problem. I'm happy to help."

They approached the apartment complex where Robert's mother lived. Liam stopped on the side of the complex's main road. He turned the engine off and cut the headlights. They sat there in the glow of a fire that was consuming part of the red brick structure. Black plumes of smoke rose into the air, devouring the buildings as it moved to the next connected two-story building. It grew by the minute. No firetrucks were in sight. In front were dozens of the creatures. They were standing in a huddle and wandering to the flames.

Sofia's eyes widened as she stared at James. "What are we going to do now?"

Chapter Three

They sat silent in Liam's S.U.V. processing the scene before them. James watched the creatures roar and roam through inches of snow. He looked at Robert in the rearview. His son's eyes were wide, and his jaw dropped. The housing court contained two rows of five connected apartment buildings. They formed a disconnected capital L shape with a walkway leading to a duplicate layout on the other side of the buildings.

Liam put his arm on the back of James' seat and peered at Robert and Sofia. "We're going to exit the car, shut the doors and move to the near side of the apartments. Okay?"

Everyone nodded and proceeded. The dog whimpered, jumped out, and raced away.

James turned. "Here boy."

The Chocolate Labrador kept running over the hill and was gone. James moved towards the others. They crossed the snowy street and crept between two of the trees that lined the sidewalk. Liam led them across the grass until they came to the row of buildings and put their backs to the red brick wall. James brought up the rear. Liam peeked around the corner to assess their next step.

He waved James closer. "Which building does his mother live?"

James pointed to the right as the flames spread from the left. "She's in the last one."

Candace's apartment was three doors down from the fire. James and Liam walked back to Sofia and Robert.

Liam glanced at him. "We've got to move without drawing attention to ourselves. The noise of the flames might attract more creatures."

James shook his head. "How will we get past the monsters?"

Robert moved beside his dad and threw up his hands. "What are we doing? We gotta save mom."

James stared at Robert. "You think I don't see that? We're trying to work out the best way to reach her without getting any of us, especially *you*, killed. Every second counts and this doesn't help. While we do this, watch for threats."

Robert glared at his father. He went to the back. Before Robert returned to his position, someone came around the edge. He slammed his back against the wall. Everyone turned. Liam drew his pistol. The figure held a gun. He was an officer. His face was clean shaven with brown hair. He was oblivious to their presence. Sweat ran down his forehead. He took deep breaths.

Liam walked towards him. "Are you injured? Hello?"

He was unresponsive.

Liam waved his hand in front of him. "Hey."

His gaze snapped to him.

Liam put the pistol in his holster and grabbed his badge. "I'm Lieutenant Smith from the Zone Seven Police Department. What's your name?"

The officer rocked. "M... my... my... my... n... na... name is..."

Sofia placed her hand on his shoulder. "Take a deep breath and relax."

He snatched away. "Don't tell me to relax! I've just watched my friends die trying to protect this place! They died protecting these people!"

James motioned for him to calm. Robert stepped back.

The officer punched the bricks. "These things can't be stopped! We weren't prepared for this! Lieutenant, what the hell are they?!"

Liam gripped his shoulders. "First thing, I need you to relax. You're scaring the lady and the kid. To be honest, you're freaking me out too."

The officer looked over his shoulder at Sofia and Robert. He nodded and took a deep breath. Liam studied his eyes. "Are you okay now?"

He acknowledged.

Liam released him. "Good. Tell me what happened here?"

The officer slid his back down the wall until he squatted. "I'm Officer Glenn from the Zone Eleven Police Department. Because of the snowstorm, a skeleton crew was at the station. A few other officers, my partner and me. Two officers on patrol spotted the creatures. They reported a ten thirty-two, all units needed. At the time of the explosions and power outages, we heard them shooting before something interrupted their transmission."

He looked up. "Everyone ran to their HoverCars, none of them would start. We traveled sixteen blocks in darkness to come here. Since these are regular roads and not heated ones, we had to hike through inches of snow. When we got here, we found their crashed vehicle in a building, but we didn't find them anywhere."

Liam and James looked around the building. Just past the mob, James saw the HoverCar halfway inside the building next to where Robert's mother lived. The HoverCar was two buildings from the blaze.

James stared at Officer Glenn. "What happened?"

He scowled at James, washed in anguish. "They didn't train us for what we faced. Nobody knows how to deal with these creatures! Plus, we were exhausted by the time we arrived. We engaged, but there were too many. I couldn't..."

He clinched his fist in anger. "Damn it! My partner is dead! I didn't even save him. He hurt his ankle when he fell. My partner reached out for help, and I left him for those monsters, so I'd survive."

Officer Glenn stared at them. "That's my girlfriend's brother. What do I tell her?"

His eyes widened. "I have to go to her!"

He moved from cover towards the street, but James grabbed him. "What are you doing? They're attracted to movement. You'll get us all killed."

He snatched away from James past the wall. "Get off me! I must protect her. They attack you, and then they suck on your neck and drain the life from you. I won't let that happen to her. Once they finish feasting..."

Claws dug into Officer Glenn's shoulders and pulled him out of sight. They stood there in shock. Liam removed his gun from its holster. He and James crept to the corner of the apartments. The creature feasted on Officer Glenn's neck while facing away from them. It dragged him backwards and spun him onto his stomach. His legs squirmed until they went limp. Liam leaned around the edge. He glanced at James and shook his head. James turned to see his son wasn't with them. He walked towards the back of the buildings. James watched Robert creeping behind bushes towards his mother's apartment via the adjacent housing court. James moved until Liam seized him. Liam pointed out the monster moving to the area.

Robert heard wood cracking and stopped. He noticed a beast in his periphery. Robert attempted to move from its path as it looked the other way. He tripped over the root of a bush and fell behind it. The creature jerked its head in his direction. Robert froze. It let loose a pulsing roar. The mob by the fire pulse roared in response. James tried to rush to Robert's aid, but Sofia and Liam grabbed him. He frowned at them.

The levees of his eyes were breaking. "I have to save him."

Sofia clutched him by the shoulders. "You will. Hold on one second, we'll help." Liam pointed to his truck. "I'll create a distraction, and then you two get him. If I can't return for you or something happens to me, go to the Zone Seven police station and find my dad. He'll help you."

James nodded. "Nothing will happen to you, but be careful."

Liam scanned the area and crept to his truck. James peered around the side and put his palm up to Robert, telling him to stay still. Robert sat frozen in the snow. The beast pulse roared again. James spotted Liam in his vehicle. The engine cut on and he pulled into the parking lot where Robert was. The monster turned from Robert's direction, let out a high pulse roar and went towards the truck. Liam turned around and drove to the main road. James and Sofia remained flat against the wall as it and Glenn's killer strode past them. He made a right onto the street and rode past the complex. The monsters by the flames shifted their attention to his vehicle and pulse roared as he sped by the residences. Their paths to Robert and his mother were now clear.

Sofia and James moved to help Robert. They advanced to the edge of the apartments. James looked at the fire, which now burned two doors from Candace's apartment and one off from the crashed police HoverCar.

He glanced around but saw no creatures. "Follow me."

They continued along buildings and turned left on the walkway. James led them to the front of Candace's building. As they stepped over the fallen door, flames dancing on the snow provided the only light. They squinted through the near darkness at the four apartments on the first floor. In the limited lighting, they observed that all the doors were off their hinges. Their eyes darted up the steps. Two larger apartments were upstairs. Creatures damaged the residence on the left. Robert ran towards his mom's apartment but slipped on blood and landed in a pool of it. As they helped him up, the thick smell of it punched them in the nose. Robert leaped over the puddle and rushed up the stairs. They followed behind him.

When they hit the top step, they gazed at his mother's brown door on the right. It was untouched. Candlelight came from inside. Robert pounded his fist.

It swung open, and his mother's boyfriend held a chrome pistol in his hand. Lex had saddle brown skin and brown eyes. He stood five feet eight inches tall with curly hair. Tattoos covered his slim body, including one on his right arm that read 'Death Before Disloyalty'. He had three tattooed tears under his right eye that symbolized the three murders he'd committed.

Robert entered the apartment. "Mom?"

His mom came out of the bedroom.

Candace had caramel skin and brown eyes. She stood five feet two inches tall and was overweight with straight shoulder length hair. Candace raced towards him, grabbed him up and kissed him on the cheek. "I was so worried about you."

As she held him by the shoulders, she saw Robert's clothes. "Oh my God. Are you hurt? What happened?"

Robert shook his head. "I'm fine. I slipped in blood when we entered the building."

She peered at the door. "Thank you for taking care of him."

James smiled. "Of course."

He and Lex stared at each other. James glanced at Candace. "We've come to get you."

He stepped towards her, but Lex blocked his path. "She's not going anywhere with you."

James eyed Candace. "Do you wanna stay here?"

Lex glared at her. She nodded. He turned around with a grin. "See? She wants to stay with me. So, you and that bitch better leave. Take your damn son with you."

James made a fist. Sofia grasped his hand.

He peered at her and then back at Lex. "Do what you want, but she dies if she stays. I can't let that happen. There's a fire two buildings away, and my child needs his parents."

Lex raised his pistol. "You're going to listen to me. I've kept her safe so far. Killed a couple of those freaks. Blam! Shot them in the face."

Lex smiled. "I think we'll go to the city. Safety in numbers and all that."

James shook his head. "That's a terrible idea. You'd be more food in one place for these creatures."

Lex lowered the pistol and punched the door with his left hand. "Shut up! I'm tired of you coming around acting like you're better than me. You don't know everything. Just because you are Middle District now doesn't make you better."

Lex glared at him. "All I heard was how I didn't compare to you in the beginning until I realized the power I had. One good slap and no more comparisons to you."

James' fist stiffened, and his face filled with anger.

Lex smirked. "I see you don't like that, but I love it."

His grip on the pistol tightened. "I won't repeat myself. Take your son, your little girlfriend, and leave."

An object struck Lex in his right arm above the elbow. He fell on his left side and the gun dropped from his hand. James rushed to grab the gun while Lex clutched his bicep. When James gazed up, Robert gripped a black metal bat with rage flaring from his eyes.

Lex groaned. "You little bastard. I'm gonna..."

James pointed the pistol at Lex. "You'll do nothing to Robert, or his mother."

He released the gun's safety. "Leave and don't return. Do I make myself clear?"

Lex scowled at James "Fine. This bitch ain't worth dying."

Lex struggled to his feet, wincing in pain. "Watch your back. This isn't over."

Lex walked down the steps and disappeared. James turned to Candace. Her hands were on her head.

Robert looked at his mom. "Lex will never touch you again."

He held out his hand. She stared at him and cried. Candace grabbed it. "I'm so sorry that I kept us in this situation. I wanted to leave; but wasn't strong as I needed to be."

Robert rubbed his mom's hand. "It's okay."

He hugged her.

Robert pulled back and looked at her. "He's gone."

She drew him closer. "I'm sorry you had to do that."

He exhaled. "Don't be. I should've done it sooner."

Candace shook her head. "Protecting you is my job."

She glanced at James. "I...."

He raised his palm.

His brow furrowed. "We'll talk later. For now, we gotta move. Some buildings are on fire. Plus, there's a police HoverCar crashed into the next one. We need to leave."

She nodded. James checked the ammo. Only one bullet remained in the chamber.

James went down the steps. "Let's go."

Robert grabbed his mother's hand while Sofia stepped beside James. They crept into the parking lot and investigated their surroundings. No monsters were in the vicinity. James studied the blaze. It reached the HoverCar.

He turned. "Move!"

The others noticed where the fire was and rushed towards the rear of the adjacent row of residences. Just as Candace cleared the side of the building, the HoverCar exploded. It blew a chunk from the left part of Candace's apartment building. Candace gawked at her home as debris fluttered in the air and the fire's intensity increased. Robert hugged his mom.

James checked the area. "That explosion will bring more of them here."

Sofia looked down the road where Liam had drawn the mob. "Do you think he's okay?" James forced a smile. "I'm sure of it. If he's dead, I'll kill him."

Sofia tried to smile back, but it transformed to terror. She pointed up the street. From the darkness, electric blue glows of death emerged. They stared at James.

Sofia gazed at him. "What do we do? They're coming."

James looked at them. "I know. I just wish we had a car that worked."

Candace pulled keys from her coat. "We can take one of Lex's cars. Would that work?"

James shook his head. "None of the HoverCars are working. The explosions seem to have fried all of them."

She handed them to him. "He drives his grandfather's old muscle cars."

James stared at the keys. '*What are the odds?*' he thought.

He turned to them. "Once we move, they'll be all over us. We need to move to the car before they get here."

They squatted and crept behind other vehicles until they arrived at the car. It was tan with chrome accents and rims. They piled in and he started the engine. James glanced in the rearview mirror. There were no creatures in the vicinity. He reversed from the parking space and shifted to drive.

The automobile jolted from an impact on the passenger side. James peered right and saw a monster unlike any he'd seen to that point. Its body was smaller than the other creatures. Less muscular but more ferocious. Its skin was glowing electric blue with navy oozing through its raised veins. The creature's eyes were regular size but still completely black. The flesh surrounding its mouth was normal, but it still bared its serrated teeth. Its beautiful blonde hair flowed in the wind. This creature was female. It cracked the windshield with a punch. Sofia scooted towards James, trying to get away from it. The monster broke through with another strike. The glass was cutting its arm, but it continued clawing for Sofia as she struggled to move aside. Blam! A bullet to the creature's head stopped it. Dark blue sprayed from the wound as it fell backwards into the snow.

The tires spun out as James slammed on the gas. When they gripped the road, he turned left at the end of Candace's lot and drove further into the sprawling complex. They headed to the opposite exit. The explosion drew monsters from the other buildings. They emerged from the woods surrounding the apartments. As he hit the apex of the hill, most of the creatures pursued them. High-pitched pulse roars filled the air. Monsters missed diving attempts as they sped by them. Going down the slope through the last winding corner, two blocked the path. One close, the other by the main street. James merged into the right lane and slid left around the curved road. The monster was getting ready to attack the vehicle. Robert smacked it with the rear driver's side door. It flew backwards as he let out laughter.

When they reached the exit, James steered hard left onto the main road to slide by the creature. It dove at them and tumbled past the vehicle.

Robert spun from the back window to his dad. "It missed!"

Sofia leaned back in the passenger seat and felt relieved.

She sat up and peered at James. "What's that sound?"

James calmed his adrenaline and focused.

A second later, he pounded the wheel. "Damn it! It didn't miss."

Candace leaned forward. "What do you mean?"

James peeked at her. "It got our tire. We're losing air."

Robert sat forward. "What now?"

Chapter Four

As they drove on the main road through the Lower District neighborhood of Dunning, James looked at them in the rearview. "We should still reach the station."

He shook his head. "Older cars have issues that HoverCars don't."

Sofia nodded. "And vice versa."

James smiled. "You just had to jinx it, Rob."

Robert glanced at him. "Sorry, dad."

James laughed. "It's okay, son."

He glanced in the mirror at Candace. James hadn't talked to her often over the past few years. They communicated through Robert about him.

James sighed. "Why didn't you tell me Lex was abusing you?"

She stared at him. "I thought you wouldn't care, considering everything. Leaving was on my mind every day, but I wasn't sure how to do it."

Candace looked out the window. "Lex was imperfect, but he loved me."

He studied her in the rearview. "That was not love. You don't destroy what you cherish. Love builds you up and makes you better. It doesn't tear you down."

James exhaled. "We haven't agreed in a long time, but you should've asked me for help. I wouldn't want that for either of you. Robert was in that."

She smiled. "Thank you Jamie."

He nodded. James turned to Sofia as she looked out the broken front passenger window into the darkness and snow.

He put his palm on her shoulder. "Are you okay?"

She stayed focused outside, but shook her head.

James glanced at her. "Are you thinking about Lydia?"

Sofia nodded.

He grabbed her hand. "If you want to talk, I'm here to listen."

She peered at him and rubbed her thumb on top of his. "Thank you."

James smiled at her and returned his focus to the street. "Damn it."

Everyone stared out the windshield. HoverCars crashed into a jackknifed cargo HoverTruck and into each other. Silence blared in their ears as they strained to hear the danger. As they surveyed the vehicle, they saw an unfriendly blue glow beneath it.

Sofia pointed. "Creatures are behind it."

James reversed to the last intersection, drove onto the wrong side of the divided highway, and sped by them. The muscle car became harder to control as the snow accumulated on the non-heated roads and the tire deflated. The monsters moved quickly towards the grass between the pavements, but they went past them.

He looked at Sofia. "We're almost there."

They returned to the correct side at the next intersection. The car swerved as they struggled to the top of the hill. As they descended, they slid down the slope.

James gripped the steering wheel. "Hold on!"

With only three inflated tires, he lost control of the muscle car as it slipped by the precinct and into a few parked vehicles. James shifted the car into park.

He turned. "Everybody okay?"

They all nodded.

As James checked the rearview, he noticed monsters making their way down the road in their direction. "Get out, now."

They exited and followed James into an adjacent alley between the red brick houses where they crashed. He picked up a large stone and went to the vehicle.

Robert reached out for him. "What are you doing?"

Candace restrained Robert from joining him. James placed it on the accelerator and shut the door. He leaned in the window and shifted it into reverse. James removed his body just before it swerved backwards uphill. It crossed the grass to the other part of the divided highway. The creatures climbed up the hill. He motioned for them to leave the alley. They moved up the long slope against the increased snowfall and faster wind. As they walked up the sidewalk, Sofia slipped, but James caught her before she fell.

Sofia smiled at him. "Thanks."

He returned the smile. "You're welcome."

She walked to his left, rubbing her arms. "I hope Liam is okay. We barely got here, and we wrecked the car."

James blew warm air into his cupped hands. "He better have. I'd hate it if something bad happened because he saved us. Liam's dad would be proud, but that's not the news I want to deliver."

She peered at him. "We didn't see his truck crashed or abandoned on the road here, so I'll take solace in that."

Robert moved to James' right. "So what's the plan?"

James placed his palm on Robert's shoulder. "We will see if Liam is here."

Robert glanced at his father. "What if he's not here?"

James stared at him. "Then we wait for a little while. Give him a chance to catch up to us."

Robert scanned the area. "Shouldn't he have arrived first? What if we're on our own?"

James turned to him. "Then we figure out how we can contact him or his father. If that doesn't work, we try to reach another station."

Robert looked at him. "Look dad, we should keep moving. Mom's here now. We should just worry about us."

James stopped. "Enough. We are not speaking negative things into existence. Bailing on him is not an option. Liam rescued all of us. Without him, we wouldn't have saved your mother in time. Leaving him isn't the man I choose to be, and it's not the person I taught you to be."

Robert's head fell. "You're right. I'm scared, and I wish we could find a bunker or something. The longer we stay in the open, the less safe we are."

James grabbed his shoulder. "Agreed, but we should stick with those who help. Good people are an asset in a dire situation. There's strength in numbers and the proud die alone. Remember that."

Robert nodded and held out his fist. James bumped it, and they blew it up. They continued up the pavement.

Candace linked arms with James as Robert and Sofia trudged forward. "How much further?"

He withdrew his arm. "Not that far."

She leaned closer. "Why did you come for me?"

James squinted at her. "You're Robert's mom. He'd never have forgiven me if we didn't get to you."

Candace frowned. "Is that the only reason?"

He chuckled. "What were you expecting?"

She glowered. "I guess I was hoping for something else as well."

James scrutinized her. *Is she thinking I want to be with her again?* he thought.

Candace pointed to Sofia. "So, why did you save her?"

He turned his head in Sofia's direction. "Are you really asking that now?"

Candace stood there.

James glared at her. "Why wouldn't I? I couldn't reach other friends in our building, but I could help her. My priority was getting Robert to safety. I saw her on the way out and she needed me. Sofia had just watched her friend die. I would not leave her. If it was Robert, wouldn't you want someone to rescue him?"

Candace nodded. He peered up the hill at Sofia, who'd stolen a look. Once they reached the intersection, they turned left.

Trees lined the road to the station and surrounded the building. As they approached, they saw a police vehicle flipped on its roof. Another laid on its side engulfed in flames. Multiple HoverCars had broken windows and windshields. Others were missing doors.

Crimson pools and trails of struggle emanated from where bodies fell in the pure white powder. Shell casings littered the ground. James scanned the location as they headed towards the building.

The station's faded black marble exterior was old and drab. Everything in Dunning felt like that when compared to the neon and holograms of the Middle District neighborhood of Morrisville. There had always been a vast discrepancy in the feel of low-income neighborhoods versus the more affluent areas. As technology grew, so did the gap.

The group moved up the front stairs. They entered through shattered glass doors. Moonlight brightened the black and white checker floor near the entrance. Broken lights hung overhead and provided no illumination. The dark within was unsettling.

James looked around the vicinity. "Hello?"

A light blue glow ignited down the hall to their left. They heard footsteps growing louder as it grew brighter. He readied himself for anything.

A figure emerged from the hallway to the right, holding an antique electric lantern. "James!"

He grinned. "Liam! You made it."

James stuck his fist out. Liam blew it up. "Of course I did. Did you think I'd bite the dust? It'll take more than a few blue freaks to stop me."

Liam knocked on the wood desk. James smirked at him.

Liam looked at James. "You can never be too careful."

Sofia walked over to him and hugged him. "I'm so glad you're fine. We worried something happened to you."

She released him, and Liam put his arms out to his sides. "All in one piece."

Sofia smiled. "That was a brave thing you did. Thank you."

He waved off her praise. "No big deal. I like you guys and might keep you around for a while."

Robert strolled over, gave Liam a five, gripped his hand, and pulled him in for a hug.

He pointed at Candace. "Liam, my mom Candace. Mom, Liam. He drew an entire group of those monsters away so we could get to you.."

Candace smiled. "Thanks for helping Robert and James rescue me."

Liam grinned. "My pleasure. It was all in a day's work."

James grabbed Liam's shoulder. "How long have you been here?"

Liam slapped him on the back. "Just got here."

James looked out the door. "Where's your truck?"

Liam sucked his teeth. "Those creatures did a number on it. Had to abandon it a couple blocks away on a side street. I walked the rest of the way."

James nodded. "Have you found your dad?"

Liam shook his head. "I was about to look. You can help me."

James scanned the area. "Where is everybody? Looks like a shootout happened in the parking lot."

Liam turned. "I'm not sure, but no body equals no proof of death. Rule number one in television dramas."

They chuckled.

Liam cleared his throat. "Okay, time to be serious again. We'll borrow firearms and plan out our next step. My father is super old fashioned, so he has more electric lanterns from the tenth century in the basement. Let's go where we shouldn't. This goes against rule number one in horror movies."

Everyone snickered. They proceeded behind Liam down the dark hall, guided only by his lantern.

James glanced at the light. "How is that still working?"

Liam studied it. "It appears the explosions affected the newer tech that relies on 6G chips. Our funding doesn't compare to middle or upper districts, so we have a ton of ancient stuff without those in them."

Liam illuminated the rooms with his gun drawn as they passed them. Each room was similar. Multiple smashed desks, blood everywhere, and destroyed equipment.

Liam glanced at James. "Looks like something stampeded through here."

They reached the stairs to the basement.

Liam turned to James. "The positive is there are no monsters on this floor yet. The negative is we don't know if there're creatures anywhere else in here."

James pointed to the roof. "Is anybody upstairs?"

Liam shrugged. "I've heard nothing since I arrived. When we reach my dad's office, I'll check his ancient satellite phone. My grandad bought three after the terrorist attacks in 2001. When they stopped making them, my old man learned how to repair them and purchased a lot of spare parts. We test them once a year when I'm on vacation for range. Dad wants to contact me in case of a major event. He always keeps one in his truck, the second here and the third at home. Plus, he collects anything antique. I assume he wants to be surrounded by things like him."

James laughed. "Hopefully it's fine since it's older tech."

Liam and James led them down the steps. As they walked, Liam filled every inch with sweeping light. When they reached the bottom, he handed the lantern to James. Liam kneeled, turned on four electric lanterns and passed them out. The lights blinded them as they hit full luminance.

Liam shielded his eyes with his arm. "That's the worse. I hate that so much."

He exhaled. "Alright, now let's get to the armory."

They nodded and followed Liam upstairs. He opened the door to the main floor and observed their surroundings. Once he confirmed the coast was still clear, they moved towards their destination. Liam ordered everyone to put their backs to the wall. He went to a huge metal door after clearing the corner. Liam unlocked the armory and froze. James peered over his shoulder and turned to shield the others from the sight. Liam went into the room.

Sofia stared at James. "What is it?"

He frowned. "There's a dead officer."

Sofia covered her mouth. Robert held Candace's hand. She drew him closer. James turned and entered.

He saw the man holding a gun. There was an exit hole in his skull. "I'm sorry buddy."

Liam sucked his teeth. "His name is Jenkins. Today was his first day. He dreamed of being on the force since high school. You know how he prepared?"

James shook his head.

Liam sighed. "Jenkins played the zombie shooter game Vile Citizen all week because the main character was a cop. He dreamed of being a hero. Life imitated art and changed the ending."

James grasped his shoulder.

Liam rose to his feet. "Let's get guns, ammo and get out of here."

He opened the weapons locker. They removed five new pistols, two shotguns, a tactical knife, all the loaded magazines they could carry and entered the hallway.

Liam assessed Robert, Sofia, and Candace. "Have any of you had weapon training?"

They shook their heads.

Robert raised his arm. "I have."

James turned. "When were you trained on shooting?"

Robert looked at them. "I wasn't. More like educated. I've played hundreds of hours of the shooter HoloGame Manifest."

Liam gawked at him. "It's not the same. Damn video games. Let me show you the basics."

He gave them a quick rundown of how to handle, aim, fire, and reload a gun.

Liam handed everyone a pistol and gave James the other shotgun. "Alright, let's find my dad and see if that relic works. If he's here, he probably made a sick last stand in his office."

Liam and James nodded to each other and cocked their shotguns.

Sofia rolled her eyes. "How many times did you practice that?"

Liam put up two fingers. "Just twice. It looked good though, right?"

She chuckled and strode away, followed by Robert and Candace.

Liam beamed at them. "Right?"

There was a loud crash upstairs.

Chapter Five

They turned off their electric lanterns and crept their way up the dark steps of the police station toward the noise. Liam led and James watched behind them. The moonlight cut through the darkness when they reached the top of the steps. A single wood wall cubicle remained standing surrounded by destruction. The glint from dozens of bullet casings lying in blood caught his eye. The smell of it hit him.

'This can't be good.' he thought.

Liam scanned the area. "I guess the battle kicked off outside and finished in here."

He inspected each of the offices while James covered him. Sofia and Candace followed, while Robert looked behind them.

Liam looked at them. "All these rooms are empty."

James put his hand on Liam's shoulder. "Are you ready?"

Liam turned from him. "You three, keep watch. Make sure nothing sneaks up on us."

Robert, Candace, and Sofia nodded. James and Liam approached the primary office at the end of the floor. They stepped over what remained of the bloody wooden desk dividers. James positioned himself to the right of the oak door when they arrived. Sofia, Robert, and Candace put their backs to the wall behind him. Liam grabbed the doorknob.

He heard movement. "Dad?"

Liam cracked the door. "Are you in here?"

It fell onto him. A creature laid on top, clawing at it.

He struggled under the weight of the door and the monster. "Shoot it!"

James kicked the beast in its side, knocking it off Liam. The creature glanced in his direction and then its head was gone. Its glow dimmed. The monster's skin appeared steel blue without luminescence. He aimed his shotgun towards the room, but it was empty.

James slowed his rapid breathing. '*I killed one of those things.*' he thought.

Liam struggled to get free. "Help me."

James put the shotgun strap over his shoulder. He and Robert lifted the door up while Liam scooted clear. They placed it on the floor.

James and Robert seized his hands and helped him stand. Liam brushed himself off. "He just had to order the heavy ass fancy door."

He entered his dad's office and paused. His father's workspace was no exception.

James surveyed the scene. '*This doesn't look good.*' he thought.

Something destroyed everything in the room. His HoloWatch, HoloPhone, and radio were smashed beyond use.

He turned to Liam. "I'm sorry."

Liam made his way to his dad's closet and grabbed a satellite phone. "For what? He's fine."

James scratched his head. "How can you be sure?"

Liam pointed to the ground. "No blood anywhere in here."

James examined the mess. "I hope you're right. If anyone deserves a win tonight, it's you. You've already risked so much for us."

Liam smiled. "I know my dad escaped from the precinct at least."

He pointed at James. "Keep an eye out while I see if this satellite phone is working."

James nodded. Sofia, Robert, and Candace entered the room and slid down its wall to rest their feet. Liam powered the phone on, but it turned off.

He put it back. "Damn."

James turned. "No power?"

Liam shook his head. "The battery drained from being stored so long. The charger appears to be at home."

Liam sighed. "My dad will come. He'll return to check for me."

Pulse roars came from outside. James motioned for Robert to guard the door. He peered out the window. "I wish he would soon. More monsters are coming uphill."

Liam joined him and pointed to the left at another blue glow. "More of them are moving downhill. I hope they just keep going and don't come this way."

Shots rang out. Candace and Sofia sprang to their feet.

James spun and glanced at Robert, Sofia, and Candace. "Watch the hallway."

He looked back outside and saw four people taking cover by the destroyed police vehicles. A bald man with beige skin in a white dress shirt with a red tie and gray pants. An old guy with alabaster skin and shoulder length silvery hair in a red jacket and jeans. A biker with cacao skin and short black hair wearing a black motorcycle jacket. And a woman with ivory skin and a brunette ponytail in her army uniform.

Liam placed his hands on his head. "Well, isn't this a shit sandwich?"

The groups of monsters merged. They stalked into the parking lot and bellowed out pulse roars. The creatures neared the group. Three of them aimed at the monsters. The guy in the dress clothes hyperventilated. Gunshots rang out, then roars and screams followed. The man wearing the tie laid lifeless in a creature's fangs. Closer to the building was the biker, also limp in another monster's grip. The older guy in the red jacket fired his sawed-off shotgun until four beasts caught him. The woman made it inside the station.

James turned. "Robert, guard the window. Candace, protect the doorway from the left. Stay low and shoot anything that comes toward this office. Liam, try to help that woman. Sofia and I will cover you."

They nodded and everyone took position. James and Sofia crept behind the only standing cubicle opposite the steps. Liam moved to the stairs and planted against the wall. The woman ran towards him. Creatures stomped after her.

Liam aimed at the landing with his weapon. "Quick, upstairs."

He heard her barreling up the stairway.

As she made it halfway, two of the monsters tackled her.

She reached for him. "Help me!"

One creature clamped down on her neck and her body went limp. Liam lowered his pistol and backed around the corner. He squeezed his left hand into a fist. The other monster stomped up the steps. Liam crept into the nearest room and grabbed shelter on the front right wall. James peeked past the divider. The creature arrived upstairs. James and Sofia aimed at the beast. He looked at Liam, who shook his head. Liam held up two fingers. James relayed the info to Sofia. Liam raised his tactical knife and waited for it to pass his hiding spot.

The creature dropped to all fours, crawled along the ground, and stopped outside Liam's location. It pulse roared. The monster scanned in James and Sofia's direction, then stepped towards them. They didn't move. Liam lifted the blade. He took a step. The beast snapped its head in his direction. He froze as it gazed at him.

James held his breath as Liam stiffened. *'Don't move.'* he thought.

A chorus of pulse roars rang in front of the building. The creature headed for the stairway. It roared as it descended the steps, which was returned by the other monsters. Liam collapsed onto his knees. He exhaled as he trembled. Sofia and James checked the stairway. The creatures were gone. They moved towards Liam.

James offered a hand. "Are you okay?"

Liam grabbed it and stood.

He stared towards the steps. "I didn't react quick enough, and that woman died. She needed me, and I couldn't save her."

Liam's head fell.

Sofia lifted his chin. "I'm sorry you couldn't rescue her, but you have saved four people tonight. That may not make it easier, but you are still our hero."

She pulled him closer and gave him a hug.

They went into his dad's office. Liam slid down the front wall near Candace and Robert to the right. James and Sofia sat on the opposite side. Liam rested in silence. Sofia peered at James. A bright light from outside filled the office.

James looked at it. '*What the hell?*' he thought.

Automatic gunfire penetrated the air, and everybody took cover.

He covered his head with his hands. '*Who is shooting?*' he thought.

Shots seemed to echo for an eternity before stopping. The quiet was deafening. James crept to look. A floodlight highlighted multiple figures who were moving toward the precinct. Creatures laid motionless in the snow. Dark blood oozed from their bodies.

He glanced at Liam. "They killed all the monsters, and now they're coming into the building."

The sound of approaching footsteps marching on the lower floor grew.

Liam wiped his face and looked at them. "Robert and Candace, one of you on each side. Sofia and James, with me. Get into position, but don't shoot. They may be friendly."

Candace glanced at him. "What if they're not?"

He took the shotgun off his shoulder. "Then we defend ourselves."

Robert and Candace got set up as James, Sofia, and Liam flipped the desk and used it as protection. They targeted at the office entrance. The footsteps ascended the stairs. Everyone focused on the door.

Liam cocked his shotgun. "I'm Lieutenant Smith. Four citizens are in here with me. Are you friend or foe?"

James was breathing slow and deep. Soldiers made their way towards them with their guns in their hands and lights on their helmets. Liam waved for them to lower their weapons.

Sofia turned to James. "We're saved!"

A squad of ten soldiers moved into two lines of five and covered the stairwell. Two men walked between them.

Liam ran towards them. "Dad!"

He gripped his father.

Liam's dad was a little shorter than him but had an extra hundred pounds of weight. His father had beige skin and was clean shaven with short gray hair. He wore his black police uniform with sunset gold accents.

His father patted him on the back. "I knew you would be fine."

Liam held his dad at arm's distance. "Likewise old man."

They both chuckled.

The soldier in winter camouflage with his father cleared his throat. "Hey Liam. Glad you're okay."

Liam looked and shook his hand. "Colonel Brian Whitehead. Thanks for taking care of this guy."

The Colonel had praline skin and had short jet-black hair. He stood about six feet tall, was muscular and clean shaven.

Brian nodded. "Anything for Isaac. He's my best friend."

Isaac grinned.

The Colonel smiled at Liam. "This place means a lot to me, but I didn't think I'd be here twice today."

Liam motioned for the rest of them to approach.

Brian peered at Isaac. "We can continue the pleasantries once we get to the transport. Let's move. It isn't safe to be out here when we don't know what we're facing."

He pointed to the steps and half of the squad brought up the rear when they moved. As they went downstairs, Liam walked with the Colonel and his dad. He stopped and inspected the area.

Isaac grabbed Liam's shoulder. "What's wrong?"

Liam pointed at the blood on the landing. "Did you see a woman laying here?"

Isaac shook his head. "No. Nobody is in the station but you."

Liam searched. "Another group was here. Three men and a woman. The guys died outside trying to fight them off, but she came in here. I saw two of them kill her and leave that stain."

Isaac grabbed Liam's other shoulder also and stared him in the eye. "No humans are out there either. You five are all that we've found since we arrived."

Liam peered at him and Brian. "Then where'd the bodies go?"

Isaac sighed. "I don't know. When they attacked the precinct, I was the only one who survived. Thankfully, I have a friend like Brian who was already coming to save us. I was alone because I couldn't protect them. Any of them."

He peered at Liam. "Where did the officer's go? When we left, the station was full of our fallen friends."

Uncertainty breezed through them more than the winter chill. As they exited the station, everyone stopped.

The Colonel removed his helmet and frowned at Liam and Isaac. "I'll top both of your questions. Where did the dead creatures go?"

Liam stared at James. "Oh hell no. We have to find a bunker. TV taught me this won't end well."

Isaac looked at Brian. "We shot several of them and scattered the rest. What happened to the ones we killed?"

The Colonel scanned the scene. "Did we kill them? What are these monsters? Can we stop them? We must go to the base and talk to General Johnson. Inform him of what we've encountered and see what's happening."

The group nodded. He signaled, and the soldiers retook their positions. Liam noticed three officers he hadn't seen in the confusion.

He leaned closer to his father and looked at them. "Who are these guys?"

Isaac's face dropped. "They're from a precinct that was attacked. We found them while we searched for you. When we heard the gunfire from this area, we rushed back."

He put his arm around Liam. "You're strong, and a survivor."

They exchanged smiles.

Liam punched his dad in the shoulder. "Just like you."

They reached the main street and looked both directions. No creatures were in the immediate vicinity. They moved across the grass divider in the middle of the road until they entered the winter camouflaged Hover Transport Unit parked at a construction site. The back wall transformed into a ramp. Two soldiers rode in front while everyone else piled in back. Liam sat beside Isaac and Brian. The officers rested by them. The squad settled opposite them. James sat in between Sofia and Robert, with Candace next to their son. Soldiers and police officers surrounded them. For the first time all night, he felt fear.

Chapter Six

The Hover Transport Unit moved above the snowy roads. The falling snow danced in the wind, illuminated by the moonlight. Darkness from the blackout surrounded them. The inside of the H.T.U. was dark gray steel. All the soldiers hung their helmets on the wall, though they held their weapons on their laps. Near the front were compartments with HoloLocks on them.

James sat there in thought. *'What if I opened our door three seconds earlier? Would that woman still be alive?'*

He looked to his right at Robert. His son's head leaned on Candace's arm as she ran her fingers through their son's hair.

'What if something happened to him before I got him to his mother? What if we didn't reach her in time?' he thought.

James observed Isaac and Liam talking.

'What if he hadn't stopped for us? I gotta repay him for that.' he thought.

He felt his left arm being grabbed and Sofia's head lying on his shoulder. *'What if I didn't see her?'* he thought.

James smiled as he eyed her face.

He pushed those thoughts away. *'I have to figure out how to continue protecting them.'* he thought.

James glanced right and caught Candace stealing looks before she turned away.

Robert leaned up and peered at his mom. "Are you okay?"

She wiped his tear. "I'm fine sweetie."

Robert's face dropped. "Are you mad at me for what I did to Lex?"

Candace beamed at him. "No, you're my hero. You rescued me. I'm not sure what would've happened if you hadn't acted. Thanks, baby."

Robert smiled. "Of course. Everyone agreed we should come to get you. I'm glad we saved you."

He laid his head back on her arm. "I love you mom."

She kissed him on the forehead. "Love you too Robby."

James watched them. *'I'm happy they're together at a time like this. They both needed this.'*

He felt Sofia shake.

James scanned the H.T.U. and spotted gray emergency wool blankets next to an officer. "Excuse me, can you throw me two of those?"

The cop tossed them to him.

He nodded "Thanks."

James handed one to Candace and Rob. He placed the other over him and Sofia. She repositioned herself under his arm and relaxed more as she warmed. James gazed at Sofia as he held her.

She smiled. "Thank you."

He brushed the hair behind her ear. "You're welcome."

James caught Candace staring at him again. She glanced elsewhere once more. He peered back towards Sofia and put his cheek against the top of her head.

***

Liam looked at Colonel Brian Whitehead and Isaac on his left. "What were those explosions earlier tonight?"

Brian took off his helmet. "I believe they were Electro Magnetic Pulse devices, but they differed from any I've seen. EMPs kill the electricity in the blast radius, but not the people. That explains the lack of death from the blasts. Our annual winter emergency drill was today. When the explosions occurred, we were outside the explosions' radiuses."

Liam snickered. "What a lucky break that was."

Brian nodded. "We jumped into the convoy and came back. Your precinct is off the highway en route to base. I had to check on your dad."

He sighed. "I didn't know there were creatures running around killing people. Nobody's prepared for this. We have no clue what's going on until we reach Shell Station."

Liam leaned backwards. "Have you contacted your superiors?"

Brian shook his head. "No. We've had communication issues as well. Our communicators work, and the base is outside the affected areas, but the towers are inside the blast zones."

He looked at the H.T.U.'s radio. "If they've passed any information on from the field, it would've been in person. They'll communicate by different means to other locations. They'll brief me upon arrival."

Isaac looked at the cops. "The officers here will do everything in our power to help. We want to protect and serve. Plus, we need retribution for our losses."

Liam and the rest of the cops nodded. '*Too many victims.*' he thought.

He eyed the police officers. "Our brothers haven't died for nothing. We'll aid in every way until we bring those responsible to justice."

Brian reached past Isaac and touched Liam's shoulder. "Let's hope we find them soon. Madmen have no place in this world."

The soldier in the passenger seat turned to Colonel Whitehead. "We're arriving at the base now, sir."

***

James felt the H.T.U. slow.

The Colonel stood. "Listen up. When we stop; follow me. I must talk to General Johnson to catch up and add the intelligence we have. Then I'll set you up with a room and a change of clothes. Understood?"

Everyone nodded. They readied themselves to exit the vehicle. It jerked to a halt. The back of the H.T.U. transformed into a ramp. The cops exited, followed by the soldiers and the civilians. As they descended, James noticed a boy racing toward them. His mother was falling behind as she chased him. He was about four years old. The boy zoomed a blue toy airplane through the air. He stopped in front of Sofia and Candace. The boy smiled at them. His smile faded as his mom grabbed him and dragged him to their tent.

James surveyed the woods around the station as snow fell and accumulated on the grass.

People and a sea of green tents surrounded them, leading to the base. *'There's at least one hundred in the vicinity.'* he thought.

He noticed bloodied and bandaged individuals. Some people cried in hysterics, while others froze in their trauma.

James saw a few sitting and rocking, muttering inaudible words.

Sofia blew warm air into her hands and glanced at James. "I wasn't expecting to see people here."

He looked at her. "Me either, but I'm thankful this many are safe. I wish there were more, and they had reasons to smile."

She nodded. They continued to follow the group through the snow and makeshift tent town. When they arrived at the gate, they moved between multiple armed soldiers in white camouflage standing guard.

James observed the four sniper towers were in the corners of the barbed wire perimeter fence.

The attached floodlights illuminated the vicinity.

The front of the building itself was light gray steel with a glass entryway. James watched Colonel Whitehead as he shook the hand of a gray-haired flattop soldier that stood over six feet tall. He was clean shaven with dark brown eyes and was muscular.

The Colonel held out his right hand. "This is General Oliver Johnson. General, my oldest friend, Captain Isaac Smith."

Isaac went to shake the General's hand. "It's so nice to meet you. Brian's told me all about you. It's like I already know you."

General Johnson chuckled. "I hope he hasn't told everything. There are embarrassing stories I'd wish to keep secret."

The trio laughed.

Colonel Whitehead pointed. "Isaac, Liam, and the other officers intend to help. They've lost good men and two stations tonight. To honor their fallen, they'll support in any way."

The General smiled. "That's honorable of you. We'll need all the help we can get to survive what's happening."

General Johnson assessed James, Robert, Candace, and Sofia. "Are these civilians with you Brian?"

Liam stepped forward. "They're with me, sir. These are my friends James, Robert, Sofia, and Candace."

The General pointed to the tents. "Most civilians are in the tents. Lucky for you four, your friend is the son of the closest friend to my second in command. Soldiers' families are in the recruit barracks. I guess we'll make an exception since you are close to family."

James walked forward and shook his hand. "Thank you General Johnson. We appreciate it."

The General looked at the Colonel. "Please escort them upstairs and then meet me in the command center. We have a lot to review. Isaac, you and the officers come with me and the squad."

James, Robert, Sofia, and Candace nodded and followed Colonel Whitehead.

As they passed General Johnson, Robert glanced at his dad. "I hope they have microbots here."

James chuckled. "I'm not sure you'll be able to play with them if they do."

Robert shrugged. "I don't have to control them. Just see them shapeshift."

They entered the glass front double doors together and proceeded towards the security checkpoint. The civilians handed over their weapons and walked through the metal detector and pat downs. Once cleared, they moved through another set of glass double doors. They walked through a short hallway that ended with a light wood accent wall in the middle with the name Shell Station in giant silver letters on it. Two openings to walk past it were on either side. To the left was another corridor. On their right were steps to the second floor. As they walked to the stairs, they saw the command center over the railing to their left. A huge hologram floated above a round table in the heart of it.

Before James got a clear look at it, the Colonel cleared his throat. "Please, follow me."

He directed them up a floating metal staircase to the right.

Once they reached the second level, Colonel Whitehead strode along the catwalk. He stopped and opened a light wood door. "I'll tell Liam where you are."

James shook his hand. "Thanks for everything."

The Colonel shook it and exited. He examined the room. It seemed like a standard soldier's space. Two light wood bunk beds on each wall fit four soldiers.

A shared living space contained a large couch and a HoloVision projector.

Each bunk had different colored army sweatsuits laid out on them and items for a shower.

Sofia glanced at the beds and then at James. "I call dibs on the shower."

James moved aside. "Be my guest. Save me some hot water."

She grinned. "I can't promise that."

Then she shut the door. He smiled. James turned and noticed Robert collapsed on a top bunk. He sat on the couch in the room's center. James rested for a minute, staring into the air. Then he took his hoodie off and rested in his undershirt and sweatpants.

Candace strode over to him. "Where are you sleeping?"

James pointed at the bed under his son. "I figure Robert and I sleep here and you and Sofia take that side."

She folded her arms. "Can we share a bed?"

He chuckled. "What? No."

Candace stroked his bicep. "I would feel safer if you were closer."

James stopped her from rubbing on him. "We're not laying down together. Soldiers are everywhere and I'm in the room if something happens. You're fine."

She sat beside him. "I'm scared, and I wanted to be more comfortable considering everything that happened tonight."

He stood. "You don't need that level of comfort."

Candace hopped up. "Well, I thought you'd care about me, given everything."

James looked at her. "Just because I won't lie with you doesn't mean I don't care. It just means I'm not sleeping next to you."

She peered at him. "What if she asked to lie with you?"

The bathroom door swung open with Sofia changed into the gray army sweatpants, t-shirt, and drying her wet hair with a towel. Candace jumped. She stared at James. Candace went to get the clothes, soap, and shampoo from her bunk. She entered the restroom and turned on the water.

Sofia went to him. "What was that?"

James checked if Robert was still asleep. '*What was that?*' he thought.

He glanced at the bathroom. "I don't know. She's never been the easiest person to understand."

They sat on James' bed.

She finished drying her hair. "So, how did you meet Candace?"

James leaned back. "We met when I was a freshman in college. She was a junior in high school. I was the youngest in my class and she was the oldest of hers, so we're only a year apart in age. Things were good at first, but things fell apart within nine months."

James sat forward. "I was getting ready to end it when she told me about the pregnancy. We were done, but nothing would stop me from being a great father."

Sofia peeked at the restroom. "I take it she did not like that decision."

He glanced at her. "She wouldn't accept it. After Robert's birth, she attempted to use Robert to manipulate me into returning. When that failed, she tried using another man to make me jealous. Then she stopped trying after a while. I believed she'd quit. Then I found someone special. Her name was Jessica."

James pictured her curly hair, her infectious smile, and her almond-shaped brown eyes. He lost days staring into them. James pictured her golden brown hand in his, and it warmed at the thought of her touch.

He smiled. "I knew she was the one in a few months, and I asked her to marry me. Candace was upset when she found out. Jess and her friends went shopping on the North Side a week before the wedding."

Tears ran down his face. "They died in the terrorist attack."

Sofia wiped them away and rubbed his left cheek.

James stared at her. '*We both lost people we loved in the same tragedy.*' he thought.

Candace exited the restroom in the tan army sweatpants and shirt. She locked eyes with James and stood still for a moment. Candace walked towards the left wall. She laid on the top bunk with her back to them. He took the black army sweatsuit and shower items off his bed.

James smiled at Sofia. "I guess it's my turn since Robert's sleep."

She nodded. He entered the bathroom and closed the door. James stepped in and set the temperature on the HoloPad. He attempted to wash away the fear and stress.

James succeeded for a moment until last year's events weighed on his mind. '*Thinking about Jess is still painful.*'

He let the warm water rain on him until it became icy. The icy water numbed his emotional pain. James exited the shower, dried off and dressed in the army sweatpants and t-shirt. As he exited the bathroom, the room was dark, and everyone was asleep. He draped the towel on a chair and moved to his bunk beneath his child on the right wall.

James went to his bed and realized Sofia was in it. "I was going to sleep over here."

He started walking to the other bunk. "I'll just..."

She grabbed his hand and pulled it. James hesitated until she tugged again. He laid down with her, and she nestled herself inside of his grasp. They drifted to sleep as Sofia lay in his arms.

Chapter Seven

The smell of fresh brewed coffee entered Liam's nostrils as he brought it to his dad and Colonel Brian. He observed a hologram projection of the county with color coded zones showing the hotspots. Soldiers moved and chatted all around him.

Liam traveled down the hallway to the first office on his left. He pushed open the ajar maple door with his foot. Isaac and Brian were engaged in conversation about the update from General Johnson. The light maple bookshelves matched the cabinets, chairs, and desk.

Isaac glanced at Colonel Brian. "This is only happening here? Nobody knows where the monsters originated?"

Liam eyed Brian '*Why here and not somewhere bigger*?' he thought.

Brian took the cup from Liam. "No idea. You at least feel rumblings beforehand about attacks or things to watch. No one heard anything of the sort. When we receive intelligence, we can stop ninety-nine percent of threats within a few days with investigation and surveillance."

Liam sipped his drink. "One percent being the bombings in Capital City and the North Side."

Brian nodded. "What happened here still sticks with me. Allegheny being bombed without warning was shocking. After that attack, we've taken steps against incidents like that ever occurring anywhere in our territories again. This... this situation is something different."

Isaac had another sip of coffee. "Thinking about dirty bombs killing all those people last year. Many first responders died that day."

Isaac looked away.

Liam grabbed his father's shoulder. "We said goodbye to a lot of great folks."

Isaac's head rose. "I apologize. The attack remains emotional for me."

Isaac cleared his throat. "Were you ever able to figure out how they moved the weapons into the city?"

Colonel Brian shook his head. "Investigators chased down leads since then with nothing to show for it. Whenever we get close, they'd end up going nowhere. Now those creatures and their origins supersede all investigations."

Liam gazed at his father. "I can't believe they did so much damage that an entire part of Allegheny is a ghost town."

Colonel Brian reclined and ran his hand through his black hair. "The crazy thing is, despite their efforts, Remnant remains floating in the air. In the wind, it floats in place. The sight is... unsettling."

Brian shuddered. "The cleaners focused on decontaminating and rebuilding closer to Downtown because of the financial significance. No money equals no taxes. Which means no reconstruction. We've only cleaned one fourth of the North Side in a year. It'll take three more years to complete the cleaning. Nobody has seen anything like this. They have to tear down one fifth of Allegheny and rebuild it. Once they understand what the terrorists used and why it's so hard to clear, the process will speed up exponentially."

Isaac shook his head. "The scientists still don't know what Remnant is?"

Brian took a sip. "Whoever created it was a genius."

They all put their cups onto the table. Liam leaned forward. "What do we understand about the monsters?"

Colonel Brian bent nearer. "From the field reports we've received, they're not too quick. The creatures glow blue, are strong as hell and vicious when they capture someone. You could outrun them, but they could catch you off-guard with a pounce. It appears they are blind and deaf."

Liam gazed into space. "A creature stared at me and didn't attack because I froze."

Brian paused for a moment. "Others have reported the same. Seems we're able to communicate near them, but not move."

Colonel Brian settled back. "From what our analysts gathered via the body cam footage we sent them, their roar acts as a motion detector."

Liam's arms flew into the air. "Hold on a second. Motion detection? Are these things lions, dolphins, or zombies?"

Brian glanced at him. "Do you always joke in tense situations?"

Liam grinned. "Yes, so my pants stay pee free."

Isaac peered at the Colonel. "Never mind him. How can we help? There are millions of civilians in this county we need to protect."

Brian stood. "I agree with you. I'll run this past General Johnson, but contacting first responders is paramount to saving lives. Killing these creatures, rescuing citizens, putting out fires caused by destruction and treating people should be our focus."

There was a knock at the door, and then a soldier entered. "The General needs you in the command center. We have a situation."

Liam and Isaac stood. The three of them emerged and walked down the corridor to the right. Liam scanned the portraits on the wall as he strolled. Each portrait was of a former Army Chief of Staff. As they approached the central projector, Liam saw a man shrouded in darkness sitting at a desk.

General Johnson held his hands behind him. "Who are you, and how did you gain access to this network?"

Liam couldn't see any details about his face.

The figure intertwined his fingers on the desk, and a disguised voice boomed through their speakers. "Who I am isn't as important as what I want. As for how I've accessed your system, I have my ways, General Johnson."

The General glared at the projection. "What do you want?"

The man tapped his fingers together. "What's best for the United Continents of America. Justice needs to rain down on the terrorists that attacked Allegheny and the Capital."

General Johnson scrutinized the image. "So, was it you that exploded nukes in the sky tonight? Or did you unleash those blue freaks that killed all those civilians?"

The individual in the hologram pounded his fist against his desk. "The Taken are the future! Those 'blue freaks' are my Reapers. My mutants are nearer to perfection than any human could ever be. You'll learn the name, then fear and respect it."

***

A booming sound jerked James awake. He leaned up in the bed.

Sofia rolled over to face him. "What is it?"

James peered at her. "I heard a loud thud, and there's a voice coming through the intercom. Something is happening."

Sofia and James climbed off the mattress and exited the room. They stood by the railings of the catwalk to watch the developments. James found Liam in the crowd. They walked down the steps and stopped next to him.

The person in the projection regained his poise. He interwove his fingers. "Losing power was a lesson that the elitist needed. Their comfort required destruction like the North Side's residents. You have ignored those Lower District citizens since the attacks. None of the Upper District citizens lifted a finger out of the goodness of their hearts. Those who helped had ulterior motives. The affluent ignore it because their loved ones weren't affected. Business continued as normal, as if it had never occurred. They walk around and flaunt their wealth and influence while those whose lives they ignored struggle to survive. Tonight, I have taken their power to show them how powerless they are. How they are ordinary, just like the rest of us when I took away their authority. A reckoning is coming for elitists and those responsible for the incidents. My Reapers will find them all and make them pay."

General Johnson looked at Colonel Brian before looking back at the caller. "What about your 'Reapers'? How were you able to create such creatures?"

The figure's distorted laugh caused chills through the command center. "Wouldn't you love that secret? Everyone has secrets they keep. That's mine. Share yours, and I'll think about sharing."

The man chuckled. "Your superior will also pay for his transgressions. Where was he when they poisoned our families? When the North Side became Dead City, why didn't he prevent it? His response was not quick enough, and he hasn't punished everyone responsible. So many individuals died, lost friends or relatives because of his lack of action. That day, they stole mi Corazón from me."

Sofia pushed past Isaac and Colonel Brian to look closer at the man's appearance. She started breathing rapidly. "Papa?"

The figure's head turned. General Johnson watched her.

She squinted at the darkness, scanning for any detail.

The communication cut off.

General Johnson eyed his technician. "Where's the transmission?"

The tech studied his screen. "I'm not sure, sir. He must have cut it off on his end."

General Johnson exhaled. "Tell me you got his location."

The soldier rotated in his seat. "We did. He's in Dead City, sir."

A hush came over the troops.

The General pounded the console. "Control yourselves. It's just the North Side. No more of this nonsense. Find out how he hacked into our base. See what he has accessed. Hack into his network and report everything you learn."

He looked towards Sofia. "You and I should have a talk."

She nodded. "Yeah... of course."

They strode down the hall with Colonel Brian and another soldier flanking them.

Sofia halted and turned. "Could James come with me?"

General Johnson smiled. "Sure."

He signaled for James to join them. James caught up with them as they headed to a meeting room.

***

Liam scratched his scalp as he observed them leaving. Isaac tapped him on the tricep and he turned.

Isaac stood there with his arms crossed. "What do you know about them?"

Liam grasped Isaac's shoulder. "Whatever their pasts are, they have done me no wrong. From my experiences with them, they're all good people. I saved them and they came looking for me."

Isaac glanced in the group's direction. "What if the girl's father is to blame for all of this? Do you think she's involved in this whole mess?"

Liam glowered at his dad. "She's not part of this. Sofia thought her parents were dead. If that is her father, his sins shouldn't condemn her. You should realize that more than anyone."

Isaac eyed him. "True enough."

He sighed. "Nor should the father's dreams become his children's burdens."

Isaac gazed at Liam. "I've been pressing too hard for you to replace me when I retire. I don't mean to be so overbearing. Even if that's my dream, I have to respect your choice."

He patted Liam's arm. "We had some tough times after your mother passed. When you became a police officer, I was so happy and honored to be your dad. I am prouder of you now. If your mom were here, she'd be proud of who you've become."

Liam beamed at his father. "Thanks dad, I appreciate the kind words. I know why you're pushing for this, and I recognize how important legacy is in our family."

Liam hesitated. "So, I accept the offer."

Isaac's jaw dropped and then a giant smile formed on it.

Liam shot a toothy grin at his father. "It won't be me that messed up the streak of Smith Captains. I can hear it already. Five Captains in a row until Liam wanted to be his own person."

Isaac pulled him in for a hug and then held him at a distance. "What made you change your mind?"

Liam nodded in the hallway's direction. "All of this and a conversation I had with James earlier. This entire night was an awakening. I am most fulfilled when I'm helping others. What better way to help than to transfer my passion for the job to generations of officers? Lead by example and change the world."

Isaac smirked at him. "Teach them everything, except your awful sense of humor."

Liam smacked his dad on the back. "Not a chance Dusty Bones. I have to share my signature trait."

They both chuckled and then Isaac slapped Liam's left shoulder.

Liam winced in pain. "Not so rough."

***

James strode through the passage beside Sofia. They followed Colonel Brian and General Johnson. Two soldiers were following them.

James watched Sofia. '*Was that really her dad?*' he thought.

The General opened a dark wood door and allowed Colonel Brian, James, and Sofia to enter. He trailed them in and shut it. General Johnson motioned for them to grab a chair. He settled next to Colonel Brian, across from Sofia and James. The General noticed Sofia's furrowed brows.

He sat upright with his fingers linked. "While that man was talking, you called him papa. After he saw you, the HoloCall ended. What makes you believe that is your father?"

Tears ran down her face. "He masked his voice, but it's what he said,"

She hesitated. "They stole mi Corazón from me."

General Johnson grabbed a tissue box from the cabinet to his rear and offered it to her. "Why is that significant?"

Sofia removed a golden oval locket from around her neck. She opened it and scrutinized the picture of her mom and dad. Sofia slid it towards the General. "That's what my father called my mother, but it's not him."

General Johnson gazed at the pictures for a minute. "Why can't it be him?"

She stared at James. "My parents died in the North Side Bombing."

The General studied her. "I am so sorry for your loss."

He returned it to her. "What do you recall about that day?"

Sofia removed a tissue, wiped her tears, and let out a sigh. "They would've been returning to their lab from lunch."

General Johnson scanned her. "What kind of laboratory?"

She put the locket back on her neck. "Dad was a Genetic Engineer, and my mom was a Neural Engineer. It was on the North Side, but they would frequent their favorite restaurant in Downtown at least twice a week. They would go there on the rail, entering and returning at Lemon Station on Kimberly Street. My mother always enjoyed that station."

Sofia smiled. "She told me it was the grandest station on either continent. I haven't seen many myself, but I can't imagine she's wrong. Marble floors and gold trim everywhere. Soaring ceilings and ivory etched walls. Super HD HoloVision stations. The smell in the food court was a mélange of delicious foods. From the sweet scent of funnel cake to the savory aroma of steak. I loved it there too."

The General stared at her. "It's possible that your parents lived if they were at the station."

Sofia jerked up her head. "What do you mean?"

General Johnson interlocked his hands in front of him. "After the bombing in the capital, we fit Lemon Station with enhancements to transform it into an impregnable bunker. We planned to enhance more stations across the continents. My boss and I picked strategic places, and Lemon Station was the first one to be upgraded. As a result, four individuals survived the strike on the train station."

She beamed, but it faded. "If they were alive, I'd have heard from them."

The General looked at them. "The attack dispersed a dangerous substance in the air. We kept survivors in quarantine to protect the public while we find a cure. I'm not sure your parents survived either, but to be thorough, what are their names?"

Sofia frowned. "Mateo and Andrea Hernandez."

General Johnson examined her. "Thank you, Sofia."

She took James' hand. "His fiancée also perished that day."

The General peered at him. "My condolences to you as well, James."

James exhaled. "Thanks, General Johnson."

The General gazed at James. "Should we search for your fiancé too?"

He glanced at General Johnson. "She went shopping at the North Shore Outlets, but if there's a chance she's living, I must know."

James stared at the ceiling. "Jessica Brown."

The General glanced at Colonel Brian. "Cross check those names with any known survivors."

The Colonel departed the office.

James placed his elbows on the table. "How'd they survive a biological attack in that station?"

General Johnson leaned closer. "If an explosion happened inside or nearby, the station seals itself. A toxic filtration system kicks on and there's no way in or out except the HoverTrain. When no further incidents transpired after an hour, we sent a train with its own purification setup to get the survivors. Medics tested and checked the citizens within before it departed to make certain they weren't a danger to anyone else."

The General sighed. "Most of them perished."

He cleared his throat. "Doctors examined and treated them monthly as a precaution. So, if they survived, we'll find out."

James reclined in his chair. "Why was Lemon Station enhanced when Allegheny had no history of attacks on that scale?"

General Johnson looked at him. "We got credible intel of an imminent attack on Capital City using nuclear weaponry."

The General frowned. "My superiors disagreed with me, but it bugged me."

He shifted in his seat. "I dispatched a squad overseas to gain intelligence against my orders."

General Johnson paused. "After the team arrived, the United Terrorist Against America discovered them infiltrating their hideout."

Sofia shifted forward. "What happened next?"

The General meshed his fingers. "A shootout occurred."

He hesitated. "The unit neutralized the extremists, but only two soldiers remained."

General Johnson straightened himself. "They verified that a nuclear missile was on a boat in international waters, close to the east coast."

He looked at Sofia and James. "Before they nullified the threat, an extremist they assumed was deceased launched it."

The General shook his head. "After killing the terrorist that started the launch, a soldier disarmed the warhead mid-flight, but couldn't stop the projectile in time before it reached the Capital."

He sighed. "It didn't take out the president or any politicians, but they killed innocent citizens."

James glanced at her, then at the General. "How does that lead to the station becoming a bunker?"

General Johnson stood up with his forearms behind his back. "Because I followed my gut, and I was correct. Much to the chagrin of Senator

Pennell. I received commendations for my bravery and protecting the President."

He paused. "I petitioned the senate to start preventative measures to protect the United Continents of America from future threats."

The General smiled. "I named it the Anti-Terrorist Initiative, or A.T.I. for short."

His smile faded. "He opposed it from the beginning."

Sofia looked at James. "Why did he oppose your proposal?"

General Johnson pointed his thumb at himself. "Because I was not a hero, in his opinion. In a closed hearing, he argued my actions almost started World War 4. I maintained my moves prevented it. The senate approved my plan, but he and his cohorts did everything to slow my progress of gaining materials and researching new tech to keep us safe. I wanted to start here and expand to other cities. We built this base and upgraded that station before the Senator tied up all the funding. The A.T.I. began research that we needed money to finish."

The General sat. "Had we got the financing I requested, the bombing wouldn't have occurred. My team would've detected the weapons using drone sweeps and random cargo inspections. Our tech could've stopped them."

He peered at Sofia. "Your family may have died because of politicians."

Colonel Brian reentered and dropped into the seat beside General Johnson. He bent over and whispered into his ear.

The General gazed at him. "Are you sure?"

He looked at her and James.

Her eyes widened. "What is it?"

Chapter Eight

Time seemed to freeze as James and Sofia waited for General Johnson's reply.

The General cleared his throat. "Seems neither your parents nor his fiancée were among those transported from the station."

Sofia sighed. James grabbed her hand and rubbed it.

She looked at him. "For a second there, I believed they made it."

James' brows raised. "So did I."

He put his other hand on top of hers *'So did I.'* he thought.

General Johnson looked at the floor. "I wish we had better news."

James exhaled. "Checking the list was worth a shot."

The General got to his feet. "Thank you for your help. Sorry we reopened old wounds. We had to confirm if it was your father."

Sofia rose to her feet. "What if it had been my dad? What would've happened then?"

General Johnson walked towards the door. "We would find him and bring him in to answer for what's transpired. Luckily, it's not your father we are pursuing after all. If you'll excuse me, I have an urgent matter to discuss. An escort will take you back. Try to rest and we'll talk in the morning."

Sofia and James departed the office. They followed the soldiers to their room.

***

Liam stood in the doorway of Colonel Brian's office. He spotted James and Sofia walking down the hall to the command center with two soldiers. James shook his head. Liam nodded in reply. He watched them ascend the steps.

Liam turned to Isaac, who sat at the desk. "It wasn't her dad."

Isaac glanced at him. "Or there's not enough proof."

Liam rotated back to the command center.

General Johnson and Colonel Brian emerged from the hallway.

The General continued moving to his office on the opposite side.

Liam glanced at his father. "Brian's headed this way."

Isaac peered in the Colonel's direction. "I'll talk to him, ask what happened and the plan going forward."

Liam smiled. "Okay pops."

Isaac rose and walked to Liam. "You should sleep. Who knows what tomorrow could bring?"

Liam chuckled. "Nah, I'm gonna stay up and go to the indoor range. I wanna be ready."

Isaac shook his head and beamed. "Are you sure that's the best idea, Captain Smith?"

Liam smirked back. "Yes former Captain Dad. Ooh! Do you think they have any experimental weapons here?"

Isaac glowered at him. "It's an army base, not the Interstellar Agency of the Americas."

Liam frowned. "Captain Party Pooper is more like it."

He headed to the shooting range on the lower level.

***

James and Sofia entered their accommodation. She walked into the bathroom and closed the door. He dropped onto his bed. James heard footsteps walking in his direction. Candace reached his side of the room and stood over him.

She whispered. "Where the hell were you?! Why'd you leave us in here alone?"

He tried to wipe fatigue off his face. "Look, a lot's happening."

Candace stomped and pointed to the room's entrance. "Forget what's going on out there. Our child needs you here."

James stood up with his hands up between them. "You need to relax. There's a building full of military personnel. I was getting more information. Me knowing the situation is me being here for Robert. Nobody's certain if this issue is short term. This may be how life is going forward. Nothing was gonna happen while I was gone."

Her eyes circled their sockets. "You don't know that. Plus, you were with her."

Candace paused. "I saw you lie with her after you denied laying with me. If you hadn't got to me earlier, would you prioritize Robert or that girl?"

She breathed hard.

He focused on her. "Is this about that?"

James exhaled. "We are not restarting our relationship."

Candace punched him in the shoulder. "This isn't about me and you. This is about your son."

He clutched his arm. "Is this about Robert, or is this about you? Last I checked, Robert has been spending increased time with me. Tonight, I saw why."

She hit his other shoulder.

James grasped that arm. "First, stop hitting me. Second, we haven't been a couple for years. Why are you so bothered by her?"

Candace dropped on his mattress and covered her face.

She wiped away her tears. "Because I see what's happening."

He scratched his skull. "What are you talking about?"

Candace sighed. "Please don't act as if you can't tell that she likes you. She's beautiful, and you like her too. I know it."

James nodded. "It's true. I do like her. She's gorgeous, and a great person, but I'm not thinking about relationships right now. Our survival is forefront in my mind. When I was engaged, you didn't act like this. What is different?"

She folded her fingers in front of her mouth. "I terminated a pregnancy with Lex because I didn't want to bring a child into that dysfunction. It was bad enough Lex was around Robert."

Candace looked down. "I always wanted to make my own family, and I was lucky that you're Robert's father. You are such a wonderful dad. When you left, I just knew we would end up back together. But you moved on, so I had to as well. You were happy, and I wasn't."

She shook her head. "Now I have so many emotional issues. I was not ready for another child, especially with Lex. You're the gold standard of fatherhood, and lord knows Lex is from the reject bin. After the abortion, I thought of you often. I regretted how I treated you. After everything that happened with him, seeing you and her like each other makes me realize how badly I messed up my chance with you. I mistreated you, took you for granted and acted as if you'd never leave. It's clear that you'll never be mine again. You'll never look at me the way you looked at Jessica. How you gaze at Sofia."

He studied her. '*I was not expecting this today.*' he thought.

Candace stared at the bathroom. "Not wanting this feeling is why I was mean when you were with Jessica. I was jealous, and I wanted you back."

She exhaled. "We won't be a couple again. I get that now. It's more about me than you or her. I realized that I have nobody."

James sat next to her. "You have Robert. He'll love you forever. Robert adores you. You have your issues, but he doesn't hold those against you."

He placed his hand on her shoulder. "Focus on you. The rest will work out. Once you are happy, you'll attract happiness into your life. Without taking care of ourselves, we can't love others."

They got to their feet.

She smiled at him. "Thanks, James, for everything. You are a great dad. Since the beginning, you've put up with my issues and been understanding. Even when I've been unbearable. If you didn't come to get me tonight, I'd be dead. He wanted to die and take me with him."

James stared at her. "I never liked him, and I told you that."

Candace gazed at the ground. Sofia exited the restroom, wiping her tears. She locked eyes with James. Candace surveyed the two of them.

He strode to the door. "I'm leaving to find Liam to train a bit more. If this situation is the new normal, I must protect my family and friends."

Sofia rose. "I'll come with you. We can practice together."

James nodded, and they left the room.

***

Isaac and Colonel Brian rested at his desk.

Brian folded his arms. "The girl's parents weren't on the list of survivors from Lemon Station. Something about it still bothers me."

Isaac reclined in his chair. "What's eating at you?"

Brian set his elbows on the desktop and interlocked his fingers. "If it's not her father, why'd the transmission end when she moved closer? I mean, it has to be somebody that is familiar with her."

Isaac shrugged his shoulders. "An uncle or family friend?"

Isaac rubbed his chin *'Someone she knows.'* he thought.

He positioned has hands behind his head. "Maybe he just figured out you were tracing his location. Several things could be possible."

Brian reclined in his chair. "You're right. If our mystery man is sophisticated enough to hack into our network, he seen us tracking him. I'm overthinking it."

'Perhaps you are more right than you realize.' Isaac thought.

He leaned forward. "Do you believe he intended to be traced? He talked to General Johnson for a while."

Brian sat up straight. "Think going after him will lead us into a trap?"

Isaac stroked his hair. "It's possible. Because we couldn't identify him, we're facing the unknown. What are his motivations? We've seen what he's created, but what led to it?"

He sighed. "Were you able to access his network?"

Brian stretched. "Not yet. We've located it but haven't cracked his firewall."

He paused for a moment. "Perhaps he wants us to come for him. It feels as if he's taunting us. I'll mention this to General Johnson."

Isaac nodded. "Not a problem. Any way we can help, we will."

Brian stood and proceeded to a light maple shelf to grab glasses.

Isaac watched as he poured bourbon into the tumblers. "Thank you Brian. Coming to help Liam and I, and General Johnson being so welcoming because of your relationship with him. Tell him I said thanks again."

Brian closed the bottle of whiskey. "I'll inform him one more time, although you have told him a dozen times at least."

They both laughed as Brian sat down once more.

Isaac reached for a glass tumbler. "When I appreciate something, I let the person know. Sometimes too often, but it's better they feel over appreciated than underappreciated."

Brian smiled, and they both sipped their drinks.

Isaac sighed in satisfaction. "That's good bourbon."

Brian nodded. "Only excellence for my honored guest."

They grinned at each other and then Brian's gaze turned reflective. "We've been through a lot of things together. Escaped the neighborhood by having each other's backs. Survived The Third War by doing the same. You saved my life not once, but twice. I wouldn't be alive if not for you. At the start of the day, I owed you two. Now I owe you one."

Isaac raised his glass. "To surviving."

They downed the rest of the whiskey and slammed the glasses on the table.

Someone knocked. Brian instructed them to enter the room. James and Sofia entered.

James glanced at both of them. "Colonel Brian, Captain Smith."

The Colonel lifted his hand. "Just call us Isaac and Brian."

James smiled. "Gotcha. Sorry to interrupt. Any idea where Liam is?"

Isaac crossed his arms. "He's at the shooting range. The three of you should rest."

James looked toward the door. "We should, but it's not a sleeping atmosphere up there. Plus, we figure we'd get more training from him."

Isaac smirked. "Ah, I see. Relieve some stress, then get shut eye. You have to stay sharp. To do that, you both need to sleep."

James grinned, and they departed the office. Brian looked at Isaac.

Isaac chuckled. "I would not want to trade places with him."

Brian laughed.

***

Sofia and James walked down the corridor towards the range. Large wooden crates of supplies that were brought from storage to accommodate the mass of people outside lined the hallway. He caught her smirking at him.

James chuckled. "What?"

Sofia held her arms behind her and skipped a step. "You think I'm gorgeous."

He stopped. "You were eavesdropping?"

She laughed. "Please. Those walls in the restroom are as thin as tissue paper. I was working to not hear you. Until I heard you say that you like me."

James' face flushed. "Well... I mean... yeah... you're cool as hell. I've had a crush on you for a minute."

Sofia pulled him along by his hand. "It's okay, I like you too. I always thought you were handsome. As we got acquainted, I sensed your sadness. I had no clue why you were sad until tonight."

She smiled. "Once you worked through that, my attraction to you was hard to keep ignoring. I was still working through losing my parents as well, but I wasn't rushing to start anything either. Now that you've rescued me, I like you more. I want to be with my hero."

He smiled at her. "Listen, with everything going on, I don't think it's the best moment to begin a relationship."

Sofia stopped and yanked him to her. She leaned up and embraced her lips against his.

Sofia pulled back and smiled at him. "This is the perfect time to start. We might not have the chance to start one later. You said it yourself, we're not sure what tomorrow will bring. Plus, this can be another reason we fight harder."

James attempted to speak, and she placed a finger on his lips. "Go with it."

She grabbed James' hand. They both beamed at each other as they strolled into the range. Liam was alone.

He spun around and saw them walk in holding hands. "Thank God. The tension was so thick between you two that it'd take explosives to break it."

James laughed. "She asked me out and gave me no choice. I'm her prisoner. Save me."

Sofia and James radiated at each other.

Liam waved his palm in the air. "Stop it... right now. That's already too much public displaying of affection with the hand holding. I can't tolerate doe eyed love gazing. Anyway, why are you here?"

She pointed her finger guns at the target. "Teach us your ways, oh great Liam. We must protect ourselves, each other, and Robert."

Liam grinned. "Alright, you crazy kids, get on over here."

He taught them everything from weapon safety to firearm maintenance. They were at it for an hour. James and Sofia yawned.

Liam scowled at them, fighting a yawn. "Stop that! It's contagious."

As quickly as they laughed, they fell to the ground as an explosion rocked the base and alarms sounded. Machine gunfire and screams saturated the atmosphere.

Liam swung around to them. "Grab ammo and let's move!"

They each snatched magazines of ammunition and ran up the stairwell, reloading their pistols. As they arrived at the end of the hallway, their faces filled with fear. A massive hole was in the wall to their left. Soldiers were firing inside the command center at Reapers.

James stared at Sofia and Liam. "Oh God."

Chapter Nine

The Reaper's blue skin glowed through the dust and smoke of the explosion. The wind brought snow in and swirled all three substances in the air. Monsters poured through the hole in the wall by the dozens as they unleashed pulse roars. James, Liam, and Sofia stepped back and ducked behind the closest two large wooden crates in the hallway.

Liam looked across the hall at Sofia and James. "We go for Robert and Candace first and then help clear out the base."

Sofia and James nodded, and the trio crept towards the mouth of the hallway, watching the carnage as they advanced. As they arrived at the rim of the command center, James saw a Reaper walking toward them from the left through the swirling particulate. He extended his arm, and they backed up against the walls. It stopped in front of them and looked in their direction. James held his breath. It stalked closer as it let out its pulsating roar. The monster twitched its head from side to side. The creature was three steps away when blue blood splattered in the middle of the corridor. It fell to the floor between them, facing James and Sofia. The mutant's glow faded, showing its blue steel skin. Liam nudged the Reaper with his foot. It didn't move. They moved to the command center.

Liam motioned to the right, and they used the faux wall with the words Shell Station as cover to make their way up the stairs. At the opposite edge of the wall, Liam peeked around it. No Reapers were in their immediate vicinity. They advanced upstairs. Liam's vision broke the top stair, and he gestured for them to halt. A creature stood in their path, facing the other direction.

Two more mutants were on the far side of the upper floor, headed towards them. James gazed past the mutant and spotted their room's broken door. He raised his pistol and shot it in the skull. It fell to the floor and lost its luminescence.

He peeked at them. "The door's busted. Stand guard while I get them."

They took their positions while James approached the room. Sofia watched the staircase while Liam observed the Reapers approaching them. James stepped over the creature and crept inside with his gun drawn. He saw items all over the ground. The couches and chairs laid scattered. The mattress was hanging off the bed, but there was no sign of Robert and Candace.

'*Oh no. I'm too late.*' he thought.

James placed his hands on his head. "Damn it!"

The bunk moved. James snapped his aim at it.

"Dad!"

He lowered his gun and ran to push the mattress. James observed Candace and Robert under the bunk. He assisted them from under it.

James gave Robert a hug. "That was pretty clever to move under there and use the mattress as cover."

Candace was shaking.

James assessed her. "Are you okay?"

She didn't respond. He glanced at Robert, who shook his head.

James set his hand on Robert's shoulder. "Good job protecting your mother."

Robert nodded.

Liam entered. "Give him a gold star later. We have to go now."

Robert grabbed Candace's hand.

James looked at them. "Advance slow and cautious."

They followed James out of the room. Liam led them to the steps. Sofia, Robert, and Candace trailed behind him. James brought up the rear. Liam signaled for them to stop at the top step. A creature at the bottom scanned away from them. He looked at James, who pointed to the two behind them. The creatures were getting closer. Liam raised his gun and aimed at the Reaper downstairs. Sofia moved to her left and pointed at one upstairs, while James targeted the other.

Liam held up three fingers and counted down to zero. All three opened fire. Sofia and Liam hit their targets in the head. James grazed the side of his target's skull. The monster became enraged and roared. It readied to pounce when Sofia blasted the creature in the head. The mutant dropped and its glow disappeared.

Sofia smiled at James. "I got you Jamie."

He grinned back at her. They all turned to the front and followed Liam down the stairs around the fallen monster. When they reached the bottom of the staircase, they stepped over another Reaper and arrived at the command center. Dead military and creatures littered the base. Others hung over half walls and control consoles. A mutant emerged from the other side of the false wall. They swung their guns as it collapsed to the floor. A giant serrated combat knife with brass knuckles on the handle stuck out of the skull.

General Johnson walked forward and took back his blade.

He pulled out a handkerchief and wiped the blue plasma off the steel. "Are you folks alright?"

Liam gave a thumbs up.

He inspected the General's weapon. "Now that's a knife."

Isaac and Colonel Brian rounded the corner.

Liam hugged his father. "Glad you're still standing old man."

Isaac patted his shoulder.

Liam reset himself. "Where are the other officers?"

Isaac cleared his throat. "Outside helping protect the citizens."

General Johnson looked at Colonel Brian. "We need to get out there and help them as well."

Then he peered at the group. "There might be more Reapers lurking, so stay alert and no sudden movements if you see one."

Liam, James, & Sofia nodded as they reloaded their weapons.

Colonel Brian looked at the pistols. "Where did you get those?"

Liam pointed behind him. "The shooting range. Figured they would be better in our possession since we love living."

Colonel Brian measured Sofia and James. "Do they understand how to use those?"

Liam grinned. "I spent the last hour training them. They already killed four tonight."

Colonel Brian sighed. "Only because you trained them. If you were anyone else, they wouldn't have those."

General Johnson went to the doorway, trailed by Colonel Brian and Isaac.

Candace leaned over near James. "What's his problem?"

James pointed to the carnage. "Well, he did just lose soldiers inside of his headquarters. He's upset at the moment."

Candace nodded. Everyone followed them to the base entrance.

When they exited the front doors, Sofia turned to James. "Where is everybody?"

James examined the area. Snow fell into the swirling wind. The barbed wire lay destroyed. He detected no Reapers, but red and blue blood covered the trampled accumulation on the ground.

They found no military or civilians.

Every person and everything disappeared.

Liam stared at Isaac. "Pops, where are all of... anybody?"

Isaac took a few steps and kneeled.

He rose with a badge in his hand, splattered with plasma. "I don't know, son."

General Johnson cleared his throat. "We are going to make our way through this encampment as a group and see if we find any survivors. Stick close, move slow and alert."

The group walked to the left half of the camp with the officers leading the citizens.

Candace's breathing became heavier.

Robert clutched her hand. "Just breathe in and exhale."

Sofia whispered in James' ear. "What's wrong with her?"

He leaned toward her. "She has terrible anxiety. We must keep her calm, or she might have a panic attack."

James peeked behind him. "It'll be okay, Candace. Do your breathing."

Candace performed her exercise. They investigated the entire camp and found nobody. Everybody stood on the camp's perimeter in silence. Sofia pushed past everyone and stooped. She paused for a moment. Sofia rotated towards James. She held a blue toy airplane, covered in blood. James' jaw dropped. Candace backpedaled toward the woods. Robert reached out for her, but she snatched away. Candace backed up further.

Robert turned to his dad. "Do something!"

James extended his arm. "Candace, calm down and do your exercise. Breathe in, breathe out."

Candace stomped with her hands at her sides. "Forget that! Children are dying! What if that was Robert?! I can't breathe! I can't breathe!!"

Candace paced along the tree line. As James moved towards her, a Reaper pounced from behind a tent onto Candace's back. It drove her to the ground face first and sank its jaws into her neck. Blood poured from the bite. Sofia covered her mouth.

Robert sprinted for her. "No!"

James restrained him. His heart dropped and his soul ached. James saw the life fading from Candace's eyes. General Johnson rushed the creature and stabbed him in the brain. In an instant, the creature's glow dulled, and the Reaper's grip loosened as it fell limp next to her. Candace laid there wheezing.

James and Robert ran over to her. Liam and the others watched the vicinity.

James applied pressure to the bite. "Don't move. We'll get you help."

Candace shook her head and cried.

Robert sobbed "You'll be alright, mom."

Candace wiped Robert's tears, but more proceeded down his cheeks.

She breathed and spoke faintly. "Robert... I love you. You are the best thing I have done in my life. Be good and listen to your father, okay?"

Tears fell from Robert's face. "I'm going to listen to both of you."

Candace pulled him closer and kissed his forehead. "Be strong. Your dad will protect you. Remember the things I taught you."

Robert nodded.

She looked at James. "Sorry for everything. Take care of our son."

James seized her hand. "I will. I promise."

Candace concentrated on the monster next to her.

She chuckled. "I told you he wanted to drag me down with him."

Candace took her last breath and was gone. Everyone walked over, and Sofia hugged Robert from behind as he cried over his mother.

James investigated the Reaper that stole Candace. "Oh my God."

Liam gazed at James. "What is it?"

James grabbed his skull. "This was her boyfriend Lex."

Robert snatched away from Sofia and scurried over on his knees. "What?!"

Liam shook his head. "How can you be certain?"

James directed their attention to his face and arm. "There's his three-tear face tattoo and a death before disloyalty tattoo on his right bicep. Lex's tattoos faded, and his hair fell out, but... it's him."

Sofia nodded in agreement.

General Johnson kneeled and investigated the body. "Are you positive?"

James eyed the Reaper. "Yes, I am."

Sofia strode over and stooped next to James. "So these creatures are... us?"

Liam scratched the back of his head. "It fits what's happened tonight. Where were the fallen officers from our precinct? What about the bodies at the station? Where is everyone that was out here?"

James glanced at Lex. "Now we understand why he calls them Reapers. They take people and make them...The Taken."

The General stood. "If they're using humans to refill their ranks, we have a bigger problem than we thought. I have to inform my superior."

Isaac scratched his head. "How will you do that?"

Colonel Brian grasped his shoulder. "That explosion destroyed our communication abilities. We must go to our sister location. Let's grab what we need and leave. Drive a Hover Transport Unit and follow us."

Isaac nodded.

James glanced at Liam. "Let's find something to carry her."

The pair searched until they found a HoverStretcher used by the paramilitary when the injured civilians arrived. They lifted her onto it from the snowy terrain and approached the building.

The group stepped over the toppled metal detectors and walked on the glass where the double doors had been.

When they came to the wall with the base name, the sign said hell Station as the S had fallen.

James sighed. '*That's correct.*' he thought.

They stopped the HoverStretcher beside the giant holographic projector in the command center. James was at the head of the stretcher, trying to warm his fingers with his breath.

James looked to his left as the General pounded his fist. "All of my soldiers are gone and all but six of the creatures. The ones we stabbed or shot in the head."

Colonel Brian peered out the door and confirmed Lex was still out there.

The General rubbed his head. "So we have to destroy the brain to put them down for good."

Liam stared at General Johnson. "Of course you do. That's where we've been aiming."

The General examined Liam. "How did you three know that?"

Liam scanned from James to the General. "Experience. James blasted one in the face outside my dad's office. It was the only one that stayed where it dropped."

Colonel Brian walked back to the group. "So these things can heal themselves after taking non headshots?"

Before anyone responded, a blue glow shone on the General. Candace sat upright and jerked her face toward Robert.

Sofia was standing behind Robert and covered his eyes to shield him from what his mother had become.

James lifted his pistol to the back of her head.

Candace turned towards him. Her skin was now blue and her eyeballs dark as the night. She kept her curly black hair and her facial structure. Candace still seemed humanlike.

He stared into her face. '*I can't do this.*' he thought.

She bared her razor-sharp teeth, and a hand grabbed her face on her right side. A massive serrated blade entered the left side. General Johnson laid her down on the HoverStretcher.

James gazed at him. "Thank you."

The General nodded as Sofia guided Robert out of the area.

Liam spun to the group. "How'd she turn so quick? Only a few minutes passed, and she already transformed?"

The General checked her. "Those are the answers we intend to find out. We need that info for projections."

James wiped his tears. "Do you have a body bag for her?"

Colonel Brian went to him. "Come on, I'll show you."

James and Liam trailed behind Brian. In front of the building, Isaac kept watch while Sofia comforted Robert. Colonel Brian rejoined them after he prepped the Hover Transport Units. Liam and James placed Candace in their H.T.U.

The pair walked back into Shell Station.

General Johnson gathered more ammunition and weapons.

Colonel Brian moved the vehicles to the building.

All except Robert and Sofia loaded the boxes of supplies and ammo.

The group piled into the vehicle being driven by Isaac. Liam sat in the front while James rested in the rear, in between Robert and Sofia. He held them both tight. The General and the Colonel lifted Lex and put him in back of their transport next to the other Reapers from inside the station.

General Johnson stood there for a few moments, staring at his base. He sighed and entered the transport driven by the Colonel. The two vehicles headed to the highway. James gazed at Sofia and Robert. He gripped them tighter. Then he gazed at Candace's body bag and thought. *'What do I do now?'*

Chapter Ten

Liam gazed out the window as Isaac drove a winter camouflaged Hover Transport Unit. He followed Colonel Brian on the dark highway as he steered the other. The vehicles moved above the snow and slush on the road. Clouds covered the moon, leaving the headlights as the only source of illumination inside the blackout areas. He gave their vehicle space but matched their insane speed.

Liam turned his gaze from the view to his father. "Why are they driving so fast?"

Isaac peeked at him and back to the highway. "With what we just learned; we have to get in contact with their superior as soon as possible."

Liam surveyed the road and looked at his dad again. "True enough, but if we cannot make it there, we can't update anyone."

Isaac sighed. "You're right. We've all lost so much tonight. That boy's mother died, and all our fellow officers perished. Our station is gone. Taken destroyed their base, and all their soldiers are deceased. All murdered, or they were ... taken."

Isaac gripped the steering wheel harder. "They wanna find the person responsible, and so do I."

Liam made a fist. "I do too. Someone must pay for all of this."

Liam viewed the passing scenery on the parkway out the passenger window. "Where are we going?"

Isaac shrugged. "I have no idea. They told me to drive this truck and follow them. It looks like we're headed back towards the city."

Sofia lifted her head from James' shoulder. "Wouldn't they have overrun Allegheny at this point?"

Liam turned. "Maybe, but I don't believe they're leading us into the city itself. At least I hope not. It'd be attempting suicide, especially with no knowledge of how terrible things are."

Isaac nodded. "It appears we're getting off at the Rockwood exit now."

Liam spun. "I wonder what experiments the scientists will run with those Reapers?"

James looked from his son to Liam. "I hope they gut them and find out everything they can, especially Lex."

Liam studied James' scowl. '*He's taking Candace's death hard.*' he thought.

James watched Robert. Sofia laid her head on James' shoulder again. She seized his hand and caressed it with her thumb. The vehicle drowned in silence as they exited the highway. Rockwood was a Lower District neighborhood comparable to Leo Creek and Dunning. Its esthetic was unchanged by the modern technology. It looked like it did thirty years ago.

They made a left onto the main street, then a right uphill. The Colonel followed the residential boulevard around the corner until they saw a shopping plaza on the left and local shops on the right.

Colonel Brian's H.T.U. stopped in front of a red brick office next to Drew's Pizza.

It had no signage, unlike the other buildings on the avenue.

Isaac pulled up behind him.

Liam observed the structure. '*What building has no windows?*' he thought.

A battered brown metal door was the façade's only feature. A light sat above it with a single security camera checking the entrants.

Liam looked at the top of the building. "This is our destination? It doesn't appear to be anything special."

Isaac put the vehicle in park. "Its appearance scares me."

The doors of the vehicles opened, and everyone exited.

They scanned the vicinity for immediate danger.

Colonel Brian and General Johnson seized Lex while James and Liam grabbed Candace's body bag.

Isaac and Sofia covered them with their guns drawn.

As they approached the door, Liam watched the camera turn to the General. '*The power is on here. How do they have electricity when the entire area doesn't?*' he thought.

A buzzer indicated the entrance was unlocked and Robert pulled the handle. They entered a hallway with glossy black walls, a mirrored ceiling, and black tile flooring. Lights hung from above every ten yards. They progressed through the long corridor until they reached the freight elevator at the end, guarded by two men in black suits, with red dress shirts and black ties. The guards held automatic rifles with both hands. They didn't move or speak as they advanced. The doors opened, and they all entered. Inside the elevator was metal with black rubber floor coverings.

General Johnson glanced at Isaac. "Press the white button."

Isaac examined the panel. A plain white button was above a basic black one. Isaac pressed it, and the elevator descended at a rapid pace until they reached their destination. The doors opened to show a giant room with white walls, ceiling, and tile floors. Another pair of armed guards wearing matching black suits, shirts, and ties stood by the freight elevator's door as they stepped out. Liam surveyed the surrounding activity. The area was full of people in white lab coats moving in all directions.

They screamed over top of each other. '*Are they scientists?*' he thought.

Straight ahead was a huge hologram projector, identical to the one at Shell Station.

A walled area occupied twenty percent of the space to their right.

It had wall-to-wall windows with three different doors.

Each door had a sign above it. '*General, Emergency, and Surgery. They have their own clinic here?*' he thought.

They moved forward to a steel desk where a man was on a HoloPhone conference call. General Johnson and Colonel Brian slammed Lex on an empty desk near a scientist, causing him to jump and scream.

The General eyed him. "Look after this, would you?"

The researcher stayed silent as he caught his breath.

His curiosity outweighed his fear.

James and Liam laid Candace's body bag on another desk.

General Johnson pointed to it. "That bag isn't to be disturbed. That's the boy's mother, and we'll bury her later. Do whatever you need to this Reaper and figure out how to cure them. There are six more in the H.T.U. in front."

Scientists ran over and analyzed Lex. On their left, glass double doors in the center of the wall led to another black hallway. The group walked through them. Rooms lined both sides as they traveled through the black hall that led to a similar space. The tile floors, walls, and ceilings were entirely black in this area. Instead of researchers, more men wearing black suits, black ties with red dress shirts sat at steel desks. A massive office mimicked the layout of the clinic straight ahead. A command center, same as the one in Shell Station, stood in the middle. They headed for the enormous office. As they arrived at the waiting area, the assistant looked at them. He was thin, in his twenties, with short brown hair, green eyes and pale skin.

The aide pointed at General Johnson and Colonel Brian. "He's expecting you two gentlemen."

The General turned to them. "Wait here."

Liam gave a thumbs up, and General Johnson and Colonel Brian entered the room. They rested in seats that lined the walls by the entrance. Liam and Isaac sat on the left wall, while James, Robert, & Sofia were on the right.

Liam inspected the floor.

He rotated to his dad. "What movie are we starring in and how do I get fired?"

Isaac squinted at him.

Liam rotated. "Where the hell are we? There are men in black everywhere with serious firepower."

Isaac shrugged. "No idea."

Liam raised one eyebrow. "Colonel Brian has never mentioned this?"

Isaac leaned closer to Liam. "Look at it. Think he'd even be able to talk about this?"

Liam smiled. "I have no clue what army protocol is. You were soldiers together, so I assumed you got a lifetime membership to knowing all the cool stuff."

Isaac chuckled. "Does this seem like a military base?"

Liam laughed.

Isaac exhaled. "Besides, you say cool, and I say it's terrifying being here."

Liam assessed the scene again. "Why? It seems interesting to me."

Isaac surveyed as well. "Whatever they discover about these creatures, there's a ninety-nine percent chance the situation is all unwelcome news for everybody."

***

James examined Robert on his right. "Hey buddy, how are you feeling?"

Robert didn't respond. James frowned and focused his attention on the office. James peered through the glass and observed a man behind a black wood desk reading his HoloPad. He was in his forties with praline skin. His hair was black and slicked back, a five o'clock shadow and deep brown eyes. He wore an all-black suit, dress shirt, and tie combo. As they stood talking to him, he continued his work. He placed the pad down and directed them to sit. As James sat there, he heard nothing from the meeting.

He leaned to Sofia and whispered. "It must be soundproof."

She nodded. "That makes sense. Look at this building. Imagine the conversations that happen in there."

James looked at her. "I'm not interested in pondering it. The details you don't have keep life simpler. With knowledge comes accountability."

James turned to Robert again. "Do you wanna talk about what happened?"

Robert shook his head.

James hugged him with his right arm. "Okay buddy. Whenever you are ready to talk, I'm here for you."

Robert peeped at him. James pulled him closer and kissed his forehead. Sofia rested her head on James' left shoulder and seized his bicep.

Liam waved Sofia and James to the left wall. He watched Robert as they walked towards him.

Liam stared at James. "How's he doing?"

James peeked at Robert. "He hasn't said a word since it happened. I've been telling him I'm here every so often, but I'm trying to give him room to process this in his own way."

Liam nodded.

The receptionist stood and departed the area.

Liam perused the window. "Did you get a glimpse of that guy?"

James glanced at the glass. "Yeah, I did. Does your dad know who he is?"

Liam squinted at his father. "No, he's never met him."

Sofia watched the floor through the glass. "It's obvious that they're scientists on the other side, but what do they understand about the Reapers already?"

James exhaled. "I hope they know tons. If not, they have six specimens now, and they better study fast."

Liam rubbed his hands together. "So, we know a headshot kills them and body shots incapacitate them for a bit. They're deaf, but they sense sustained movement. That they were human. What else do you think they'll learn from them?"

James shrugged. "No clue. I expect they'll analyze their makeup and create a cure. Nobody should have to witness their family turn into that. No one should have to end their relative's life."

Sofia assessed James' face. "Do you believe a treatment is possible?"

James gazed back at her. "I remember when HoverCars and holograms were fantasies. Anything's probable if those are real. If any place can achieve it, this facility is our best shot."

The General and Colonel exited the office. The group rotated.

Liam pointed at the room. "Who's that guy?"

General Johnson smiled. "That's my superior, Mr. White. He runs this operation."

James examined the floor through the window. "What is all this?"

Colonel Brian stepped forward. "This is The Agency. We lead when the United Continents of America deal with the unknown."

Sofia cocked her head to the left. "What type of things do you investigate?"

Colonel Brian scanned her face. "The Reapers, the chemical used in the North Side bombing known as Remnant. Stuff like that. They've been researching the substance and any aftereffects on the environment since the incident. Doctors also studied the four survivors of the attack."

James looked at him. "Did they discover anything about Remnant?"

The Colonel nodded. "After studying those four, we collected samples of their blood to make a vaccine. In theory, it immunizes you to it."

Sofia's eyebrows raised. "Why is that necessary?"

General Johnson stepped forward. "Soon people will start moving into the cleaned sections of Allegheny's North Side. This inoculation should make them immune to trace levels that may remain. In theory, a larger dose might help against higher concentrations of exposure."

The General looked at Colonel Brian. "I guess we're about to find out."

Liam glowered at them. "What does that mean?"

General Johnson placed both hands behind him. "Mr. White tasked us with going to Allegheny's North Side and catching the man responsible. They've taken too many citizens and turned them into Reapers."

Liam whispered to James. "It's a very vicious cycle."

Isaac glared at him.

The General cleared his throat. "If we're unsuccessful in ending this, it'll be a pandemic within days. We brought the bodies of those six Reapers here for further study. Good thing we did. We sent teams to capture a few of them earlier, but they haven't checked in yet."

Isaac stepped towards Brian. "Let's take it to these bastards. Where are we rendezvousing with other stations?"

Colonel Brian grasped Isaac's shoulder. "There are no other bases. They were all attacked. Some troops were on patrol, but they never reported."

Isaac peered at him. "Well, did they try to communicate with the other police departments?"

Brian nodded. "They did. We've got no responses from them either. They tried to contact everyone. The operation is on the two of us. We're awaiting help from other cities and states, but they may not arrive in time to stop this from escalating."

Isaac crossed his arms. "It can't only be the pair of you. That'll be a suicide mission. What about the agents here?"

The General looked at Isaac. "They are the contingency plan. If we don't complete our objective, they could be all that stands between two million Reapers and the rest of the continents."

General Johnson sighed. "Sitting idle and doing nothing while the numbers of the enemy grow to an unstoppable number is suicide. Millions of citizens dwell in the city. The army can't beat that amount of Reapers. For every person we lose, their totals grow."

Isaac glanced at them both. "So, it's decided?"

General Johnson nodded.

Colonel Brian smiled. "Yes. I want backup, but I couldn't live with the thought of that many deaths while I'm able to help and waited for reinforcements."

Isaac unfolded his arms. "I understand why you are doing it. You should've asked for my support. I'm coming with you."

Brian held up his hand. "I appreciate the offer, but I'd never ask you to put yourself at this much risk. Think of your son."

Liam waved. "I'm standing right here. Plus, if dad's leaving, I'm going. You'll need our help. I am not a bench rider, I'm the star player coach. So... I'm putting myself in the game."

Colonel Brian stared at General Johnson.

The General peered at both officers. "Returning from this mission isn't likely. Succeeding is even less probable. The odds are not in our favor. Are you certain you want to do this?"

Isaac and Liam shared a glance.

Isaac peered at the General. "Yes sir, we're sure."

General Johnson showed the armory's location. "Go equip yourselves. We leave in fifteen minutes."

The General and the Colonel left.

Liam looked at James. "Are you coming with us?"

Isaac crossed his arms. "James is staying here. He has Robert to consider."

James looked at Isaac. "That's why I'm going with you."

Isaac scowled at him. "If I die out there, my son is already a grown man. If you're killed, yours is a teenager, and he still needs you."

James clutched Isaac's shoulder. "If I sit here, do nothing and you all fail, then I haven't protected Robert by doing everything possible. How many other fathers saved not only their children, but other kids tonight? Who would I be if I stayed and did nothing?"

Sofia styled her hair in a ponytail. "I'm not staying either."

They all stared at her. Isaac glowered at her.

James eyed Sofia. "Are you sure about going?"

She grinned. "Just because I'm a woman does not mean I'm not courageous. Yeah, I'm scared, but courage is being frightened and still doing it. I have to protect you. Like you're attempting to protect us. I like you, and I wanna see where this goes. Plus, the Reapers murdered my best friend earlier. It's time to get the person responsible."

James smiled at her. She returned one of her own.

"They killed my mom."

Everyone spun and saw Robert standing there. "I won't sit here like a little kid when I can help. If numbers increase the chance of success, then our odds got better, right?"

Isaac sighed. "I recognize the anger about your mother. Being angry is justified, but this mission is too dangerous."

He glowered at James and Sofia. "This mission is unsafe for all of you."

James inspected Robert's eyes for a moment. *'Do I allow him to go or tell him to stay?'* he thought.

Isaac glared at James. "You cannot lead your son into this situation. It's way too risky."

James gazed at his son. "He's young, but Robert's making a selfless decision. Those creatures killed his mother. Plus, he has already saved my life once tonight. Perhaps he can aid in saving millions more. Besides," James watched Mr. White's office. "I'd feel better about him being with me than in here."

James waved Robert closer. He grabbed his left shoulder before staring at him. "You stay attentive and listen to everything the General says. This is real danger, not a game. Do you understand?"

Robert nodded. Sofia and Liam each put an arm around him, and they headed to choose their equipment.

Isaac grasped James' tricep. "I hope you know what you're doing. You're endangering them both."

James stared at him. "I hope I do too. They both volunteered to do this. I rather they stay here too, but I'm just following my instincts."

He patted Isaac's grip on his arm, and the Captain released him. James joined Liam, Sofia, and Robert at the weapons depot. Colonel Brian and General Johnson entered the armory. The General walked next to James. "What are you three doing in here?"

James finished loading the magazine and slid it into the gun. "Giving you backup. You need all our help. Besides, we've survived so far."

The General observed him for a second. "Brian and I will do our best to defend you, but your job is to make sure that boy stays alive. We are doing this, so kids like him have a future. Remember that the goal is priority over everybody, even me."

James nodded, and they both finished equipping their weapons.

Chapter Eleven

They waited by the elevator dressed in advanced biochemical resistant bodysuits.

Unlike standard hazmat suits, these were formfitting with higher levels of resistance.

The uniforms contained multiple anti tear fabric layers.

They wore enhanced HoloWatch like communicators on their wrists.

Their helmets had built in breathing masks to protect them from Remnant.

James, Liam, and Sofia received proprietary weaponry that favored energy and chemicals over projectiles.

Liam took a Sonic Shotgun that would tear a Reaper to pieces at close range with sonic force.

The shotgun was white with a clear panel in the middle which showed the inner black barrel. The end of it was a single enlarged hole.

James received an automatic Shock Rifle. It connected every two sharp rods fired via a wire that conducted an electric current upon the impact of the second rod. Effective for taking on multiple enemies. The top was steel blue. From the trigger down was black.

They gave Sofia an Acid Pistol which shot small green acidic balls using air pressure that dissolved on impacting the target.

The barrel and grip were transparent, while the rest of the firearm comprised a shiny gray polymer.

Isaac refused an upgraded weapon.

They handed Robert a standard silenced handgun, as they did everyone, in case of another electromagnetic pulse.

General Johnson stood before them with Colonel Brian. "You stand before us today as a pair of officers of the law and a trio of courageous citizens. The mission we are about to embark on is dangerous. It's also an operation that may save millions of people. That's the only reason we permitted you three civilians to go. We might fail the mission. Last chance to withdraw."

Nobody budged.

The General looked at them. "Have you all received your Remnant vaccine?"

Everyone nodded.

Liam grabbed his left shoulder. "Did they have to push so deep?"

Isaac glowered at him.

General Johnson scanned everybody. "Okay then. Let's get moving. Follow me."

They entered the freight elevator, and the General rested his finger on the black button. A blue light scanned his body from top to bottom.

A few beeps sounded, and a voice spoke. "Identity confirmed." They seemed to descend for an eternity before the doors opened. A blast of warm air hit them. Two armed guards in biochemical bodysuits watched for threats. In front of them was a platform and a black armored HoverTrain above the track.

'Looks like it's built for hauling materials, not people.' James thought.

He examined the roof of the train station. *'We are far below street level.'* he thought.

This area looked industrial.

James found no marble or gold anywhere, just concrete.

As they approached the train, James glanced down and saw yellow residue near the tracks. '*What is that stuff*?' he thought.

He nudged Liam. Liam viewed it too before peering at General Johnson. James looked around the area. '*Where are the workers?*' he thought.

The General typed his code to enter the train as Sofia and the others observed. It powered on, and the second car's doors opened. General Johnson and Colonel Brian entered first as the group followed behind them. The Colonel headed to the controls of the HoverTrain and put it in motion. All of them sat on the hard metal seats.

Liam leaned forward with his hands folded, hanging between his legs. "So, is this your personal train? I didn't think Generals had these kinds of perks. Must be nice during rush hour."

The General smiled at him. "Only in my dreams. This has a more practical use. You can't transport hazardous material through city streets or on public trains. We needed to gather Remnant from Lemon Station for study to find a cure. So, we used this train."

Liam glanced out the window. "So, did you rush and build this track, or was it already here?"

General Johnson rested back in his seat. "How do you believe the government transports weapons of mass destruction? By HoverCar in traffic surrounded by unpredictable civilian drivers and hackable self-driving cars? Or in the cargo of a vulnerable autonomous commercial flight? How about using unmanned choppers over the city?"

He smiled. "This track's been here for years. We've also equipped this HoverTrain with a failsafe."

James sat forward. "Where were all the workers? The floor's super busy, but only the guards are down here."

General Johnson pointed. "Everybody we have is upstairs, considering our situation. Researchers are working to discover how he created Reapers so they can create a treatment. Reversing what he's done is the goal. Hopefully, they'll find one soon. Who knows how long the continents could survive without it. Everyone else is part of the contingency plans should we fail."

Sofia leaned forward. "Are there other places like The Agency where soldiers report?"

The General chuckled. "No other place is like The Agency. In a code black, it becomes the base of operations for both continents. If you can get here, you do. If not, you travel to a station in the next safe zone. Hopefully, they made it to the other protected zones with no issues."

Liam extended his hand. "Since The Agency is the primary hub, is Mr. White in charge?"

A hologram of Mr. White sitting at his desk appeared before them. "You all are very inquisitive."

Liam jumped out of his seat. "Don't do that!"

Mr. White smiled. "You are correct. I run point on everything going on in these sensitive situations."

Liam pointed to his communicator. "Were you listening this whole time?"

Mr. White nodded. "Yes, I oversee critical missions like this. Too much is at stake for me to sit idle."

Liam peered at him. "What do you mean by sensitive situations?"

Mr. White folded his hands on his desk. "Anything that surpasses our knowledge or isn't normal. Things that would terrify the public. Those are the issues that I handle, along with omega level national security threats."

Sofia glanced at James and then at Mr. White again. "What threats are those?"

Mr. White shook his head. "I can't tell you. The one reason you're there and General Johnson was forthcoming is because you've lived this nightmare already and survived so far. We'll debrief you; have you sign nondisclosure agreements and such once you stop the man responsible. Whatever we learn from your experiences will be vital. Besides, seven people are better than two."

Liam stared at Mr. White. "Who's your boss?"

He chuckled. "You don't need to know. It isn't necessary to complete your job. Appreciate the fact that I've kept you safe from things before tonight you'd only seen in your nightmares."

The group was silent as they exchanged looks.

Isaac stared at him. "So, what is the plan?"

Mr. White reclined in the chair and picked up his drink. "Once you reach your destination, you'll make your way to street level. Once there, move on foot towards the suspect's location."

He sipped his bourbon and put the glass on the desk. "You civilians are brave. This is a courageous thing you're doing. I'll chime in when needed."

Liam took his communicator off and assessed it. "How do I block incoming HoloCalls on this device?"

Mr. White grinned. "You can't. Just think of me as your holographic assistant."

The hologram disappeared.

Liam mouthed to James. "He's creepy."

The loudspeaker buzzed. "I saw that."

Liam inspected the train until he found the camera.

He pointed at it. "Look, big brother, we need to set boundaries."

Mr. White chuckled, and the speaker went silent. The HoverTrain climbed up a steep hill.

Colonel Brian looked at them. "We're making our final approach to the location. It's time to ready yourselves."

Everybody nodded and turned their attention to the front of the train. General Johnson got up, and each person joined him.

He held up a fistful of dog tags. "These men were military. When a threat emerged, they sprang to action to combat it. They let go of their sense of self-preservation to protect others. These soldiers fought until the very end. Their sacrifices gave us the opportunity to get to this point. They did not die in vain."

He scanned their faces. "You are now soldiers. Danger is calling still, and you sprang into action to fight it yet again. You are putting each other and many lives ahead of your own. We'll battle and win. I won't lose another soldier tonight. Stay focused and watch each other's backs and we'll survive. We will carry out our mission, alright?"

Liam gave a thumbs up. The General and Isaac walked over and talked to Colonel Brian. James, Robert, Liam, and Sofia said a prayer of protection. The General rotated and observed it. They concluded praying and checked their weapons.

General Johnson grasped his rifle. "We've arrived."

They slowed to a halt. The iron shutters sealed the station exits. A bright pink forcefield accompanied them. The General turned on the exterior lights. James gasped as illumination filled the train station. A yellow pollen like substance was sitting in the air. Some pieces were small as snowflakes, while others were palm size. They all trailed General Johnson off the HoverTrain.

James checked the vicinity. "What is this stuff?"

The General pushed a few stationary baseball sized pieces aside. "This is Remnant. The residue of the chemical used in the bombings a year ago. Since we continue to clean and study the material, spores still float in place where we haven't reached. We use this station to transport materials to The Agency. Our cleaning crew will scrub this route last."

James looked at him. "Why haven't we heard about this?"

General Johnson looked at him. "Do you think the public would stay calm if they saw this? That's why we built the wall surrounding the North Side. Only people working with The Agency enter."

Liam shook his head. "How much Remnant is remaining?"

The Colonel nodded "A lot. The bombing was worse than what we told the public. After a year of cleanup, seventy-five percent of the North Side still has Remnant everywhere."

Isaac watched him. "How much worse are we talking?"

Mr. White's hologram popped up in front of them. He removed the cigar from his mouth. "It's classified. Know that everything is being done to finish as soon as possible. Unexpected complications arose."

A howl emanated from deep in the tunnels. Everyone looked in that direction. A giant metal door sealed the tunnel.

Liam peered at Mr. White. "Something's in there."

Mr. White picked his cigar up and puffed it. "Then it's best that you go ahead with your mission then."

James peeked from Mr. White. He observed Sofia looking at the HoverTrain station. James moved to her and grabbed her hand.

She squeezed it. "We're here."

Tears ran down her face. "This is where my parents died."

He pulled her closer and hugged her.

The General went over and touched her back. "I'm sorry for bringing you here, but Lemon Station is the closest to our destination."

Mr. White cleared his throat. "Let me remind you all you are in enemy territory. Stay vigilant, so you make it home."

General Johnson turned and glared at Mr. White before his hologram disappeared once again.

He looked her in the eyes. "Are you ready?"

Sofia took a deep breath. "Yes, I am."

He looked at the others. "Let's clear this train station before we do anything else. Liam, James, and Robert with me. Isaac and Sofia with Brian."

The group split into their assigned squads. They proceeded to opposite ends of the train station. The General put his back on the security office's right wall. James, Robert, and Liam stacked up across from him. He signaled for Liam to open the door. Liam opened it as General Johnson powered on the light, stepped through the doorway, and walked left. Liam trailed and cleared the right. Robert and James were the final two inside the room.

The General glanced at them. "This office is empty."

James advanced and leaned over the wood desk. "General, you may wanna come and look at this."

General Johnson strode over and inspected the papers. "What the hell?"

He lifted a scattered pile and placed them on the desk.

The General picked up one sheet. "They will all pay. That's repeated on all these."

James examined them closer. "Who wrote these?"

General Johnson studied the page. "I'm not sure."

Liam showed stains on the sheets. "A few papers have smears of blood on them. You think Reapers attacked them?"

The General turned to Liam. "That, or maybe they were the attacker. It appears whoever did this, they're long gone."

Liam looked at James. "Who even uses paper anymore besides the dinosaur I call father?"

General Johnson peeked up at them. "Let's meet up with everybody at the exit and move out."

They exited the office. When they stopped, the General watched Colonel Brian approach. "Did you uncover something?"

The Colonel shook his head. "We found nothing. How about you?"

General Johnson glanced backward. "Just babble from someone who was down here writing they will all pay on paper. The sheets had parts covered in blood. No signs of the writer being here anytime recent."

The General stepped up and rotated to the group. "Listen close. We are in a known area in an unknown situation. There's no intel about how many Reapers are here, so stay alert. I want Isaac and Brian in the rear, watching our backs. Liam and I will lead. If I say halt, you do it. If I tell you to run, you do it. Follow my orders, or you may die. Is that understood?"

They all nodded at him, and General Johnson ascended the steps. At the top, Colonel Brian approached the terminal and input his code as Sofia and the rest watched. Another howl emanated from the distant darkness of the tunnel. They all scanned the HoverTrain station. The General and the Colonel exchanged glances. Everybody turned back to the gate.

Before he pressed enter, General Johnson eyed them. "The movement can attract any nearby Reapers. They could be on the other side, so be ready."

Everyone took a side of the steel gate and aimed. Sweat trickled down James' face. His heart raced as the energy field disappeared. The gate lifted halfway and stopped. His finger rested near the trigger. Liam and the General exited first. The civilians followed, with Colonel Brian and Isaac tailing. They investigated the blacked-out area.

General Johnson peered at each person as he lowered his gun to chest level. "Clear for now. Keep your eyes and ears open for any light or movement."

They moved down the middle of the street in darkness. The lights inside and on the sides of their helmets lit up their faces and the area. The General and Liam were clearing every alley in both directions as they progressed. Isaac and the Colonel were walking backwards, doing the same. James was busy watching the rooftops through the Remnant for movement.

Sofia looked also before turning to him. "Do you see anything up there?"

James kept scanning the roofs. "Nothing. I figure I should watch high while they cover street level. You can't be too safe when you recognize the real danger that surrounds you."

Sofia tapped her helmet. "Good idea."

She gazed past him to Robert.

Sofia strode up to his left. "How are you feeling?"

Robert shrugged. "Sad and angry at the same time. All I know is the man responsible for my mom's death needs to suffer the way she did."

James went to his son's right.

He grasped Robert's shoulder. "I understand your anger about your mother. We'll hold the guilty party accountable for what he's done, but they won't pay by your hand. I do not wish that for you."

He snatched away from his dad. "I don't care what you want. This is what I want. He took my mom. That murderer cannot go unpunished."

General Johnson stopped and turned to Robert. "The courts will punish him. Trust me, he'll answer for all lives lost, not only your mother's. He may be the key to reverse engineering a cure. Murder is the last thing you need on your conscious. It never leaves you lonely. Especially if that act condemns the United Continents of America to this fate."

The General gazed at the unit. "Let me reiterate, we kill any Reapers, but we capture the man responsible."

He stared at Robert. "That's nonnegotiable. Do I make myself clear?"

The group nodded.

General Johnson waved them onward. "Good. Our first stop is close."

After taking a few more steps, James grabbed Liam and pointed. "Look up there."

Everybody halted and stared at the apartment rooftop behind them to the left. A glowing figure stood there, but it didn't glow blue. This creature glowed red. Its arm raised towards them. Reapers jumped from windows, broke down the front doors of that building and ran at the group.

The General beckoned them. "This way!"

They sprinted down the street and burst into their destination. The group followed General Johnson between dual rows of three desks for the rear wall. James faced the door and gripped his Shock Rifle. He aimed at it and prepared for a breach. The General touched his communicator and the back wall lifted to show a small space and a metallic door. James spun around and ducked under it with the others. Once everyone crossed under the faux wall, General Johnson started lockdown. A bright pink forcefield activated at the entrance, then a steel gate lowered from the ceiling. A second forcefield started by the false wall as it dropped. James bent over to catch his breath. The General moved to the door.

As he approached, blue lights scanned him. The door buzzed. "Identity authenticated."

It swung open.

General Johnson held his right arm out. "We'll be more comfortable in the office."

One by one, they entered. The door shut as Reapers threw themselves through the front windows and against the forcefield. They heard the loud banging as they tried to break through the barriers. After a few moments, the pounding stopped.

Liam gazed at him. "What the hell was that red Taken?"

The General shook his head. "I don't know."

Chapter Twelve

James examined the office. A cherry wood shelf full of books was on the left wall and pictures hung on the rear wall. In the front corners of the room were two United Continents of America flags. A medal display hung on the right wall. The General sat behind a matching cherry wood desk as Colonel Brian and Isaac rested in the chairs on the other side of it. Sofia and Robert relaxed against the right wall.

Liam paced across the office. "So let me get this straight. Not only do we have blind hyper aggressive blue Reapers, but now there's red Taken who can see and guide them?!"

He turned to the Colonel. "Did you know more kinds of Taken existed?"

Brian shook his head. "We knew as much as you did. This complicates things."

Sofia held up her hands. "How was nobody aware of a new Taken until this moment?"

The General extended his hand. "We are the second group of people to enter this area tonight. They lost contact with the first squad. Maybe they haven't sent the red Taken outside the North Side."

James looked at Liam. "Why keep them here?"

General Johnson rubbed his chin. "Why indeed?"

Mr. White's hologram of him sitting at his desk appeared behind Isaac and Colonel Brian. "That's untrue."

The General leaned over the desk. "What do you mean it's not true?"

Mr. White sipped from his glass. "The team that we sent there when you detected the hacking activity informed me of the latest Taken. They made it a little past where you stand before we lost communication. Red Taken are irrelevant if you stay alert. The plan is still the same. Catch the person responsible and extract them via HoverCopter. Destroy all data once we download copies."

General Johnson slammed his fist on the desk. "Why weren't we made aware of this before we engaged on this mission? For us to be successful, we need all available intel. A Taken variant with vision is relevant."

The General glared at him. "Anything else you'd like to share?"

Mr. White leaned closer. "The information was need to know."

General Johnson reddened. "We needed that info. There are more dangerous Taken than we've already fought. Taking on Reapers that can't see is one thing. Overcoming them when they're being directed by a new Taken is a whole new challenge. Something more aid would help with."

Mr. White smiled. "This development creates another wrinkle, but one you can handle. You two are the best soldiers we have. The officers you have with you are excellent. I don't care how you do it, just get it done. You are to focus on your task."

The General gritted his teeth. "Yes sir."

Mr. White reclined and folded his hands. "Good."

Then his hologram disappeared.

Liam pointed his finger to where Mr. White vanished. "This is my problem with this situation. I can't believe..."

He paused before moving towards a picture that sat on the shelf.

Liam held the photo up and peered at General Johnson. "Is this your office?"

In the picture, the General was smiling with a couple of teenage girls around a dinner table.

One had brown hair, porcelain skin, and blue eyes.

The other had blonde hair, green eyes, and warm ivory skin.

Everybody turned to General Johnson.

He nodded. "It was when I wasn't at Shell Station. They moved me here after the Capital City attack to oversee Lemon Station's enhancements."

James stared at the photograph. *'The brunette looks familiar.'* he thought.

Sofia looked at them. "Were you here when the attack happened?"

Colonel Brian moved forward. "We both were."

Attention shifted to him.

He glanced around the room. "We worked in this office when we heard rumors of a plot. Our entire team of soldiers walked the streets in plain clothes, trying to find anything or anyone suspicious. The General and I were meeting in the front office as the bombs exploded."

Colonel Brian peered at Isaac. "The news only reported one explosion, but multiple occurred. The explosions pushed the yellow particles we now call Remnant into the air. We moved to the door, but not knowing what Remnant was, we kept it closed. People ran from it, died right on the sidewalk. We didn't know how to help or if we could. Before it froze in place, Remnant moved fast and came under the door. So, we ran into this office, which doubles as a bunker. It has its own limited oxygen supply in case of emergency, so we stayed in here."

He scanned the room. "We also lost soldiers that day. People with families. This operation means a lot to us too. We failed them once here, and we don't intend to fail them again."

Liam held up his arm. "If you had dwindling air, how did you escape without being exposed to Remnant?"

General Johnson took the picture from Liam.

He smirked before looking at him. "The same way we're leaving now."

The General moved a few books and pressed the button they hid. They heard a metallic click and then the rear bookshelf swung open to reveal concrete stairs in front of them that descended into a passageway.

General Johnson held out his arm. "Follow me please."

One by one, they passed him until they all were in the tunnel, and he shut the bookshelf door behind them.

As they walked down the steps, Sofia leaned closer to James. "I don't like this. Why'd Mr. White hide that detail?"

James peeked left at her. "I don't know, but something's wrong with that guy. It's almost as if he wants the mission to fail."

He looked down the long tunnel. The floor, walls, and ceiling were all concrete. Strip lights on both sides of the roof lit the passageway. Robert walked to Sofia's left. Captain Smith and Colonel Brian walked behind them. General Johnson and Liam approached on his right.

Liam stared at the General "Who are the girls in the photo?"

General Johnson sighed. "The brunette is my daughter, Olivia. The redhead girl is her best friend, Judy. Olivia was home when the attack happened. We had a huge fight that morning over her getting a tattoo."

He glanced at Liam. "I wasn't even mad about the ink. An operation that didn't go according to plan upset me. One of my top soldiers died on that mission. I was angry at myself and transferred it to her over something so trivial."

The General sighed. "When the oxygen in the safe room ran out, we traveled through these tunnels. We had no clue if they would be toxin free, but they were. When I got beyond the contaminated area, I made my way home. When I arrived, she was gone."

He looked at Liam and James. "I lost my daughter over an argument that I blew out of proportion. After her mother's death, I did that plenty. I searched for her, but I didn't find her. Nor did I reach Judy either to see if she knew where Olivia was."

General Johnson paused. "I still haven't found her, but I believe she is safe wherever she is."

James turned to him. "I hope you're right, but how do you know?"

The General stared at him. "It's something that I can't explain. I just feel it. She probably doesn't want to be located. One day we'll reunite. Once we finish this mission, I'll try to find her once more. First, I must rid the world of the current threat, or what's the point of finding her to bring her into this hell?"

James and Liam nodded.

Isaac eyed the Colonel. "How far does this hallway go? I might die if we continue too long."

Brian slapped him on the back. "You gotta hit the gym."

Isaac laughed. "This is just desk weight. I'm all muscle underneath it all."

Brian chuckled. "Remember the New Roads Project?"

Isaac glanced at him. "The plan to fix the crumbling streets of Allegheny?"

Brian nodded. "The government used that opportunity to build a series of tunnels called The Web under the streets for quick transportation."

Isaac stared at the Colonel. "Where do they lead?"

Brian pointed to the red steel door coming into focus. "There, among other places."

He approached the concrete wall on the door's right as General Johnson advanced to the left. A light projected blue HoloKeys onto the surfaces. They both input codes. Sofia and the others observed as the door lifted.

The General held out an arm. "Welcome to The Warehouse."

James inspected the massive location as they entered. Metal shelves rose to the high ceiling, filled with giant wooden crates. He looked at Liam. "What is this place?"

Liam aimed his helmet's light at a container with the words 'Property of the United Continents of America' written on it.

He scanned the soldiers. "A shady government facility, obviously."

James leaned closer. "Why is it under a neighborhood?"

Liam shook his head. "That's an excellent question."

He walked beside General Johnson. "Why is this hidden below the streets of a neighborhood? What's so special about this location?"

The General smiled. "Allow me to ask you something. What arrived first, the best research universities on the continents or items that needed researched?"

Liam glowered at him. "I hate riddles. What is all this stuff?"

Mr. White's hologram appeared. "Things above your pay grade."

Liam glared at him. "Listen here pal, I'm not getting paid for this."

He eyed James. "Are you receiving compensation for this?"

Mr. White sneered. "You are here because a problem needs fixing, and you have proven yourself a capable tool. Nothing more. So, stop asking questions you don't need the answers for to do your job."

Liam saluted. "Yes sir, Mr. Shite. Tool man out."

Mr. White stared at him before his hologram vanished.

General Johnson placed his hand on Liam's shoulder. "Trust me when I tell you this. He isn't someone you want as an enemy."

Liam crossed his arms. "Mr. White started it."

He looked around the area. "So, what's the plan from here?"

The General pointed to the opposite part of The Warehouse. "When we exit, we'll be a few blocks from our target."

Liam turned to James. "Very convenient."

The sound of boxes being smashed ended James' laughter.

General Johnson waved everyone to crouch. "Stay low and quiet. Brian, kill the lights. We're not alone in here."

Colonel Brian entered a command on his modified HoloWatch, and the lights went out. The General took the lead, and the group trailed in formation down an aisle. They crept from lane to lane towards the exit on the far side. As they strolled closer, they saw blue glows moving through the surrounding aisles. General Johnson raised a fist, and they held in the middle of a lane. A Reaper walked behind them from their right to the end of their aisle. It spun in the opposite direction. Another appeared in front of them from their left towards the other end of the aisle. James tapped The General and showed him an empty bottom shelf next to them. General Johnson stepped through, and everyone followed as the Reaper reached their lane. They pushed forward, but stopped again. The Reaper that passed behind them reached their new aisle. The creature let out a pulse roar. It jerked its face around for a second, waiting to pick up movement. They stood deadly still. The Reaper moved past their aisle. They breathed a collective sigh of relief.

Liam leaned nearer to James and whispered, "That was close."

They heard an additional creature approaching in front of them. James concentrated on that side, expecting to glimpse the other Reaper. A red Taken strode into the lane. Its eyes weren't completely black; they were bright yellow with black pupils. The red Taken's upper body was not muscular like its blue brethren. It paused at the aisle's opening, peering at them. Then it grinned.

Liam groaned. "Oh hell no."

He shot its chest with his silenced pistol multiple times. It let out a shriek. As it fell, it crashed into wooden boxes, knocking them against the floor. The Reaper that moved past the lane behind them came back. They froze. It traveled past them. A pair of Reapers advanced from the other direction. They went to the cry's source.

The Reapers circled the fallen red Taken.

James watched closer. *'They almost look concerned.'* he thought.

Two of the Reapers backed off and one of them approached the collapsed red Taken. It sank its fangs into its neck. The group gasped.

James' eyes widened. *'They feed on each other?'* he thought.

He saw the red Taken's veins darken. The Reaper stepped backward, and the other Taken writhed in pain. Its back arched, and everyone slowly raised their guns. The once diminutive Taken sprouted muscles. Its color also changed to purple.

It rolled over onto a foot and a knee, then stood. The red Taken now more resembled a Reaper.

It had a Reaper's physique with glowing purple skin.

The creature kept its bright yellow eyes and black pupils. It stared at them.

It smiled at them a second time. "Get them."

Liam aimed his gun. "Kill it! Kill it dead!"

They opened fire. The twice-mutated creature ducked and ran away as the Reapers moved towards them. One of the creatures leaped at them. Liam blew its head off with his Sonic Shotgun. He stepped aside, and the body thudded where he stood. James hit the torso and face of another with twenty electric rods from his Shock Rifle. It twisted in pain until it budged no more. Colonel Brian double tapped it with a head shot from his silent pistol. Sofia took down the third by peppering its body with acid rounds. Holes burned into the Reaper's flesh until it fell to the ground. She finished it with an acid pellet to the back of the skull. The vibrancy of their glows faded, and their skin grew dull.

James scanned the darkness in a circle. "I don't see any Taken."

Liam bent over and tried to catch his breath. "Hey, Mr. Shite, what in the hell just happened?"

Mr. White's hologram appeared. "You got up close and personal with a Thinker."

Liam stood up, gasping for air with his hands on his head. "Thinker?"

Mr. White drank his bourbon. "That's what we're calling them. They're distinct from Reapers as far as physiology is concerned. Thinkers have vision, but don't seem as strong. They don't appear to be mindless and feral, hence the name."

James raised his hands. "How can they mutate each other? Mutating people is crazy, transforming themselves into other variations is terrifying."

Mr. White nodded. "Reapers differ from humans; thus, they can alter us. They're also different from Thinkers; so the former can modify the latter. At least that's our current logic."

General Johnson looked at the fallen creatures. "So, we have three variations? Two that have vision and lead Reapers."

Mr. White stared at him. "That's correct."

The General nodded. "Understood. They were here when we arrived. Maybe the Thinker was looking for something. We're about to investigate now."

Mr. White peered at him. "The contents of certain crates are highly classified. Make sure nothing is missing and look inside alone."

General Johnson scanned everyone. "Yes, sir."

Mr. White's hologram disappeared.

Liam shook his head. "I thought Mr. White was about to let me into the flock."

The General strode for the exit. "Follow me and stay sharp."

They followed behind him.

Liam glanced at James. "If the red ones are Thinkers, do we name the purple Taken Evolved Thinkers?"

James shrugged. "At that point, you might as well call them humans."

Liam stopped. "You just blew my mind."

Colonel Brian walked by him. "Let's go."

Liam moved again. They found three metal crates with their tops ripped off in the center of The Warehouse. The Colonel positioned himself between the group and General Johnson. The General proceeded and peered inside the crates. At the third crate, he froze for a moment. He hurried to grab the lid of the crate and fumbled it as he placed it back on top. General Johnson made a private HoloCall to Mr. White.

He hastened to them and pointed past the boxes. "Let's move out at once."

The group followed.

Liam leaned towards James. "What's in the box?"

James shrugged. "Whatever it is, it shook him."

They stopped at The Warehouse's exit, staring at the raised red metal door. The General lifted the modified HoloWatch on his left arm and moved through the menu of holograms until he halted at one. He stared at it for a moment.

General Johnson turned. "Few people know The Warehouse exists. Plus, it requires double authentication to enter. Those creatures didn't wander in here. They were let inside."

Isaac pointed to the hologram. "Who would let them in there?"

The General cleared his throat. "Her parents."

Everybody spun around to Sofia.

She covered her mouth. "That's impossible. They're supposed to be dead."

Chapter Thirteen

The group stopped near The Warehouse's red metal exit door, staring at Sofia.

She stood there looking at General Johnson. "How can my parents be alive?"

The General closed the door and walked down the tunnel. "That's a question we'll both ask them when we get there. The location of that hack is close. That isn't a coincidence. They knew about this facility. His reaction when he saw you makes sense. Our instincts were right."

Everyone followed in tow.

Sofia rushed up beside him. "How would my mom and dad know about this place?"

General Johnson stared straight ahead. "We've worked together occasionally. Your parents researched sensitive government projects. With his ability in Genetic Engineering and her skill in Neural Engineering, everything fits. He changed them physically while she altered their sensory systems."

Sofia blocked his path forward. "You knew my parents, and you didn't tell me?"

General Johnson stared into her eyes. "We knew each other a long time ago. That information wasn't necessary."

She shook her head. "Now it's a necessity?"

He nodded. "Since we discovered they're responsible."

Sofia glanced at the floor. "How are they alive? They weren't on the survivors list from Lemon Station."

He laid his palm on her shoulder. "I'm not sure. We'll find out when we arrive."

General Johnson stepped around her and kept moving down the hallway. Isaac eyed Sofia as he walked by her. Sofia and James approached each other. She gripped him tighter, and he held her close.

Tears streamed down her face. "How were they alive since the bombing and they didn't return to me? Why not tell me they're okay?"

She released him. "What if my parents are responsible?"

He grabbed her hand. "I don't have the answer to either of those questions. But I'll be beside you when you ask. Let's get those for you."

Sofia's expression turned from confusion to anger.

She quickened her pace and strode away.

Isaac waited for James to catch up, then he sidled up to him. "Do you think she knew, or is she innocent?"

He paused and turned to Isaac. "There's no way she was involved. Plus, I wouldn't tell her about this plan if I were her parents. You'd only put her in danger."

James caught up to Sofia.

Liam strolled up to Isaac. "She's blameless dad. Her mother and father are guilty, but Sofia isn't."

He glanced at his son. "We'll see soon enough."

Isaac marched away. Liam stared at him and then followed. The team reached a GravLift that required dual identification to activate. General Johnson and Colonel Brian once again input their codes as Sofia and the others observed. The lift powered on, and they entered in groups. They ascended to the top floor.

Once the last group left the lift, they approached a gold metallic wall that raised to reveal an office.

They walked out onto black marble floors with golden specks.

The twin floor to ceiling windows had gold trim.

One overlooked Allegheny's North Side, while the other looked toward Downtown. The destroyed modern glass and steel desk lay in shards, and the crystal chandelier hung crooked. James examined the door and glimpsed a large metal gate above the entryway.

Brian peered at the General. "Do you think he didn't have time to lower it?"

General Johnson glanced at him. "Based on what we understand, I bet he did, but raised it when he saw a couple of familiar faces."

Sofia looked at him. "How are my parents involved with him?"

He peeked at her. "It's a long story that I can't tell you. I'm sorry."

They exited into a waiting room where the flipped secretary's desk and scattered seats littered the space. Some chairs were on their sides, the remaining lay broken. They departed the reception area and stepped into a luxurious hallway. The flooring and the windows matched the office.

The General peered at the unit. "It looks like they've been here with the Taken. Stay alert for any surprises."

The group nodded, and they moved down the hall, checking each room along the route. They moved toward the lift at the end of the corridor. Everyone entered the GravLift in groups until Isaac and Liam remained.

He glanced at his dad. "Not one more damn lift."

Isaac shot him an expression. Liam got in and they traveled down to the lobby. Once they joined the group, Colonel Brian and General Johnson walked onward. The rest of them trailed and scanned the space. Everything looked clear. The foyer was enormous, with windows that started on the ground and ended at the second floor ceiling of the two-story open area.

A gold escalator ascended to level two. Super High Definition HoloVision stations lined the first floor.

Liam stopped in his tracks. "What are we doing in this building?"

He pointed at the logo on the marble flooring. A black circle with gold trim enclosed the golden letters L and I. "Why are we at Lincoln Industries?"

The General beckoned him to follow. "We can walk and talk. There is no time to waste. They may already be gone, or we will just miss them because we're standing here chatting."

Liam moved, and they headed to the exit.

Mr. White's hologram appeared next to them. "Jack Lincoln is the richest man in the city. Money, power, and influence are vital when you are trying to save the world from unexpected threats. Similar to what we face tonight."

Liam chuckled. "So, is he the hero in this story? Or is it you?"

Mr. White shook his head. "I never said I was a good guy, but I am on the continent's side. This evening, it's the living, the humans versus the Taken. The soldiers you're with are the heroes. They have done thankless things to keep you safe and they're about to do it once more."

Liam slow clapped. "That was beautiful. Will you write the next speech I give at a middle school?"

Mr. White disappeared.

He looked at his dad. "I guess that was a no."

The group exited the property with caution. They were almost at the contaminated zone. Their side of the street was the New North Side. With renovated or new buildings. Inches of snow blanketed the road. Dead City was across the boulevard. Comprised abandoned structures and particulate. Remnant hung in the air but stayed over that sidewalk, as if an invisible barrier kept it back. From the sunset gold contagion came a doe and a pair of fawns. The groups exchanged stares as they passed each other. Liam watched the deer with suspicion.

James felt a rush of warmth as they penetrated the contamination zone.

He glimpsed at Liam and Sofia. "Is it me, or did it just get warmer?"

She peered at him. "It's not you. I feel it too."

Robert agreed. "Why is it warm in a blizzard?"

Liam pointed to the pavement. "Notice any snow on the sidewalk?"

James looked at the concrete. "No. What's going on?"

Sofia nudged him and directed his gaze at an orange brick building on her right. "This stuff is all over the buildings. It almost seems like... the Remnant is spreading."

He stared at the abandoned properties. It covered a few. Others were husks of themselves, filled with their destroyed remains from the explosions. The damaged structures sat boarded up and wrapped in scorch marks.

James looked at Sofia. "How can this neighborhood look like this a year later? This is crazy."

She nodded her head. "Agreed."

He gazed behind them. "The difference in the reconstruction and what remains unfixed is... staggering. It's surreal to have a clean area across the street."

Liam stared at Lincoln Tower. "Think about this. That skyscraper did not exist before the bombing. They built it after the attack last year once they cleaned this section. His donation paid for half the cleaning and revitalization. That didn't even dent his change jar."

He eyed the General. "Now we realize why. I believed he did it because he loved this city. Instead, he improved security for the Ark of the Covenant below people's homes. What is he getting from this?"

General Johnson motioned for them to continue walking. "He deserves a lot of thanks and gratitude. The government had to respond. The extended cleanup is also their responsibility, but politicians tied up the rest of the funding. They were attempting to earmark their own causes into it. That's holding up the money. His contribution merits whatever he wants. I recognize everything has a price, but where would we be without him? Businesses would not have reopened on the New North Side if he did not announce Lincoln Tower first. Plus, devoid of his donation, half the rebuilding would still need finished."

The General stared at Liam. "He put his own money in, so I'm fine if he profits later."

He stepped in the General's path. "What was in the box? You seemed disturbed by its contents."

General Johnson grabbed his shoulder. "With The Warehouse, believe me when I tell you this. You don't want to know what I do. Some details keep me up at night."

The General tapped his HoloWatch. "Plus, I couldn't show it if I wanted to, and I do not. That's me doing you a favor."

General Johnson went around him and shook his head. "I wish I didn't see it."

James exchanged worried looks with Liam as he strode by, with Sofia and Robert flanking him.

Isaac waited for Liam to walk beside him. "Would you stop giving General Johnson a tough time and focus?"

Liam's jaw dropped. "He said 'Trust me,'. You never believe someone who says that."

Isaac glowered at him. "We're unfamiliar with the situation we are about to walk into when we reach the location. You are supposed to be a captain when I retire. Start acting like one and stop behaving like a petulant child."

Liam held up his finger. "Hold on a second. This is me. Who I've always been. What is your problem?"

Isaac pointed to the neighborhood. "My problem is we may not survive this situation alive, and I need to see that you are taking this seriously."

Liam peered at him. "I'm still standing, am I not? Just because I joke, or question authority, doesn't mean that I take things lightly. You should understand that more than anybody. I thought you did."

He studied Isaac's eyes. "Maybe I was wrong."

Isaac interrupted Liam by grabbing his shoulder as he attempted to stroll past him. "You weren't mistaken. I love you and I want to make sure you're ready. We've faced nothing that compares to this. Nobody has. There are several unknowns in this situation. Don't let hubris be your downfall."

Liam smirked. "I love you too dad. It won't get the best of me because I, for one, am not arrogant. There's a purpose behind my actions. You must allow me to be who I am. The man that you taught. Trust your teachings as a father, and as an officer."

Isaac nodded as he placed his hand on Liam's helmet near his cheek. He smiled at him. His son grinned. They hurried to catch up with the squad, who'd stopped at the edge of an intersection. Isaac patted Liam on the back and they both readied their weapons.

General Johnson waited just outside the heaviest contaminated location.

Colonel Brian was beside him while Robert, James, and Sofia were in the middle.

Isaac and Liam were in the rear.

The General spun to face them. "Cut the chatter and stay alert. We must focus more than we ever have in our lives."

The group refocused. General Johnson led them into the Remnant. The yellow particles were denser here. He and the officers cleared the alleys and scanned structures for any threat. The three civilians did the same.

James looked at Robert. '*I have a lot to lose if the operation is unsuccessful.*' he thought.

He stared at Sofia. '*I also have plenty to gain if we succeed.*' he pondered.

General Johnson steered their attention down the boulevard as they continued. "Once we turn left at the upcoming intersection, the destination is straight ahead."

The unit nodded and proceeded. General Johnson turned the corner, but he slammed his back against the wall. The rest of them did the same. Remnant exploded off the bricks into hundreds of little yellow pieces that froze midair after 3 seconds. James inspected where they smashed into the wall. The space refilled itself. He pointed it out to Liam.

Liam focused. "What the hell?"

He pulled at his father.

Isaac snatched his arm away. "Not now."

Colonel Brian leaned forward. "What is it?"

General Johnson glanced at him. "A mass of Reapers are in front of the structure."

Liam looked at James. "Of course. Why wouldn't there be?"

Isaac leaned closer. "What's the plan?"

The General peered at Liam and Brian. "You two scout and report back. Move around that building to give yourselves an extra block of safety from any Thinkers seeing you."

Isaac stared at his son. "Be careful."

He smiled. "When am I not?"

Isaac frowned at him.

***

Liam followed Colonel Brian up the adjacent alley to the far corner of the building to get a better view.

The Colonel touched his helmet. "Zoom in, times two."

Liam gaped at him. "These helmets are voice controlled? Why was I not informed?"

Brian glanced at him before covering his eyes. "Zoom out! Zoom out!"

He caught his breath. "That was frightening."

Liam rolled his eyes. "What are you implying about my appearance?"

Colonel Brian narrowed his gaze. "You weren't told because the knowledge was not pertinent. Surprise. Stop complaining."

Liam squinted back at him.

The Colonel looked at the structure again and touched the side of his helmet. "Zoom in, times two."

Liam crouched closer. "What do you detect?"

Brian continued to scan. "The General was correct. There are too many Reapers by the building's entrance. There are less on the building's flanks. Regular view."

He glanced at Liam. "Do you suppose the rear is a viable way, seeing as the bulk of them are in front?"

Liam shrugged. "It might be a workable approach, or a trick."

Brian nodded. "It may be a trap, but I still like those odds more than fighting through the Taken."

Liam stared at him. "It's the better choice. At least we understand an ambush awaits."

The Colonel turned to the building and zoomed in again. "Let's look at the roof."

He examined it for a few seconds, sweeping from left to right. "There are three Thinkers on the rooftop. One in front, and a couple on the sides. Toward the back is clear."

Liam shook his head. "It's definitely a trap. The Thinkers are thinking."

Brian stared at him. He glanced at the building again.

The Colonel squinted. "Zoom in, times two. Take a picture. Regular view."

Colonel Brian returned to cover, extending his arm to pull Liam back around as well.

Liam eyed him. "What is it?"

The Colonel exhaled. "We have to return right now."

They stood and returned to the group.

The General watched them approach. "What did you see Brian?"

Brian glanced at him. "Just as you said. A crowd of Reapers were in front and on the sides of the structure. There appear to be fewer in the rear."

Liam raised a finger. "Looks to be a ruse. They're begging for us to approach that way."

Brian nodded. "It's possible, but it's our best shot. There is also a trio of Thinkers on the rooftop. None towards the back."

The General looked at Liam. "Trap or not, we go where less resistance and a higher probability of success are."

General Johnson stepped forward and then Colonel Brian moved into his path. "There's one more thing."

The General observed him intently. "What is it?"

The Colonel cleared his throat. "When I viewed the structure again after surveying the roof, something in the building caught my eye."

General Johnson peered at him. "What did you glimpse?"

Brian projected the hologram in front of them. "Her father seen me with binoculars. They know we're coming."

Chapter Fourteen

They stood at an intersection in Dead City with Remnant all around, a few blocks from their target. The group paused there, looking at the hologram of Sofia's father. James grabbed her left hand with his right. He rubbed her thumb with his.

Sofia gazed at the projection. "Did you see my mother?"

Colonel Brian looked at her. "No, I only saw him staring back at me."

James caressed her back. "She has to be there with him. Your mom was the other authorized person to open The Warehouse."

Isaac stepped forward. "If he knows we're coming, why hasn't he sent the Reapers after us yet?"

General Johnson pointed to Sofia. "Maybe he assumes we have her here, which may help us."

Isaac advanced. "Should we be taking Sofia along? Why not use her as a bargaining chip if things go bad?"

Sofia scowled at him. "I'm not leverage to be used as you choose."

The General put his hands out to diffuse the situation. "She's right. Sofia could be the key to prevent this mission from going awry. She may facilitate all of us surviving this."

Isaac stared at her for a moment before nodding.

General Johnson eyed the group. "Alright folks, let's retrace our steps and go down a couple of blocks on a parallel street. We'll avoid the Taken and approach the building's back entrance."

The General raised his finger as Liam elevated his. "We know it's a trap, which means we have an advantage in expecting the unexpected. Remain focused and stay safe."

Liam dropped his arm. The unit nodded and followed General Johnson as he turned in the direction they approached. They made a right at the previous intersection and moved down a few blocks. The blue luminosity of the Reapers' skin on the parallel road shone through the narrow alleys as they traveled until the Reapers were out of sight. They went right again and pushed towards the structure's rear entrance.

The group arrived behind the building across the street from their destination. They observed the back of their target.

General Johnson, Colonel Brian, & Isaac planted against the corner.

The Remnant that covered the structure exploded into hundreds of yellow pieces once more.

Liam pushed them away from his face. "Please stop doing that. Plus, I'd get clear of the wall. That stuff grows back. It has to be why cleanup is taking longer than expected."

The three backed off and saw the healing transpire.

Colonel Brian tapped his communicator. "Record that."

Liam gaped at the Colonel.

Brian pointed to his helmet. "Video archive."

Liam turned to James. "They're not getting this outfit from me."

James studied the structure. The tower was white and thinned near the top. It featured black tinted ShadeGlass on every floor except the lobby. Across from them was a wide metal garage gate, and a red door up a small set of stairs. The area was clear. The General inspected the intersection to their right. All the Reapers faced the opposite direction. He examined the roof but didn't detect the Thinker who was there prior. General Johnson signaled for them to move, and he protected them as they crept across the road. Once they crossed, Brian covered his approach. When the General reached them, Brian approached the security box on the ceiling close to the rear door. He interfaced his modified HoloWatch with it and the door opened.

Liam pointed. "Can I keep this stuff when we're done saving the world? This is so cool and would be a glorious reward."

Mr. White's hologram appeared in front of them. "No."

The image disappeared.

Liam glanced at James. "He's so stingy."

General Johnson entered first. Two lights on his headgear switched on and burned through the darkness. He took a few steps forward. The rest of the group followed, and their lights pierced the darkness. A pulsing hum of a massive power source, heat, and pitch blackness greeted them. The door shut behind Liam. General Johnson moved closer and hesitated. His light revealed someone kneeling in blood. The figure looked at them.

General Johnson strapped his shotgun to his shoulder. "Jack?"

He rushed ahead. The gagged man grunted. A bright blue shimmer flashed before General Johnson. It hurled him backwards to the floor. The General stood up and advanced to the forcefield. He reached out his hand. It pushed his forearm back once again. The space before him rippled with blue waves that disappeared in the air.

The General surveyed left to right. "What the hell?"

Claps came from the shadows. "How do you like my forcefield? Don't waste your time searching for a weakness. My barrier is stronger than the ones you use. You won't get into this half of the garage."

They raised their guns and turned to the person.

The figure held up his palm. "I wouldn't do that if I were you. Go ahead if you want bullets ricocheting everywhere. It makes no difference to me.

You'd just save me the hassle of having to kill you. That would be more efficient, and I prize efficiency."

Liam aimed his helmet beams into the man's eyes.

The figure shielded his face. "Don't aim those into my eyeballs. Allow me to help you."

The room's lights filled the space. They stood on the platform in an empty loading area. Parked vans sat to their left. Sofia gasped.

General Johnson gripped his rifle tighter. "Mateo Hernandez. Exactly who I wanted to see. I saw that you and your wife paid a visit to The Warehouse. Where is she? I would love to say hello."

Mateo was a forty-nine-year-old Colombian. He stood five feet eleven inches, average physique, with black hair and brown eyes. Mateo wore a black lab coat with rolled sleeves, a black polo shirt, and gray dress pants.

He positioned his arms behind him. "You mean for old times' sake?"

Mateo smiled. "She's upstairs. You will see her soon."

Sofia stepped forward. "How are you alive?"

Mateo grinned at her. "Hola mi Princesa."

Tears ran down her face. "Do not my princess me! Why did you let me think you're dead? What are you doing here? Are you responsible for the things that they're blaming on you?"

He shook his head. "Don't blame me. Life dealt me terrible cards, and I decided they needed changing."

Sofia crossed her arms. "How is unleashing these Taken not your fault? Your monsters are infecting innocent people."

Mateo waved a finger. "I'm evolving them into superior beings. Making the weak powerful."

She stared at him. "This is not okay papa. You can't do this to anyone without their permission."

He laughed. "Evolution does not ask for consent, it just happens. The fragile will evolve or die, while the wicked perish."

General Johnson strode nearer. "Free Jack Lincoln now."

Mateo smirked. "I won't be releasing him. Look around Oliver. Do you believe you are controlling anything here?"

Colonel Brian stepped forward. "Why did you kidnap Mr. Lincoln?"

Mateo encircled his hostage, who squirmed from him.

He stared at the Colonel. "Jack is here to answer for his crimes against me, Allegheny, and humanity. I'm glad you are here for this sentencing."

Brian glanced at General Johnson and then Mateo. "You are not a judge. The authority to choose people's fates is not yours."

Mateo stopped and glared at them. "I do not follow your laws anymore. Justice is now created by me, as I've designed my own beings. I am master of the new civilization. You'll view firsthand what happens to people who wrong me."

Liam stepped forward. "How has Mr. Lincoln wronged you?"

Mateo strolled closer to the blue forcefield. "He has harmed not only me, but the United Continents of America and humanity itself."

Liam peered at Jack Lincoln and lowered his weapon. "What did he do?"

Mateo went towards his daughter. "One year ago, bombs exploded on the North Side."

General Johnson grunted. "We all are familiar with the attack. It's old news at this point."

Mateo snapped his gaze to the General. "Everyone knows they attacked us. Is everybody aware of why?"

General Johnson gritted his teeth. "That's the one thing we haven't been able to uncover."

Mateo sneered. "Well, it looks as if I've done your job for you. Relax while I tell the story. Since you're unable to hinder me from doing so from where you stand, you will."

Colonel Brian, the General, and Isaac kept their weapons aimed at Mateo. James, Robert, and Sofia held their firearms by their sides.

Mateo scanned from right to left, then focused his attention on General Johnson. "Last year, my wife and I were returning to this lab from lunch at our favorite restaurant. She wanted to take a half day. I insisted we return and continue working on a special project."

His brow furrowed. "I should have listened to her. She often came second to my work. Barely, but second. She agreed to go back to the lab. I was lagging as we exited the train. A man bumped into me while I was studying my notes. I dropped the HoloPad with my research on it. As he ran outside, I noticed a tattoo on his neck. A very distinct design. I picked up my pad and looked for her. Andrea was on her HoloWatch, close to the exit. She didn't witness this transpire. I tried to catch up with her through the crowds. Just as she walked out, an explosion happened outside the station."

Mateo studied Sofia's visage before staring back at General Johnson. "The blast threw everybody backwards. Yellow particles burst into the terminal. I scrambled to my feet and rushed to her. What I glimpsed was not good. Your mama was unresponsive, and I thought I was losing her. Her pulse was faint. Screams came from every direction, but the yells inside my soul were loudest. I feared I would lose mi Corazón."

He concentrated on Sofia. "I knew that for her to survive, we had to reach the lab. Seeing her like that, I realized she had little time. The loudspeaker announced lockdown procedures had started. I lifted her up in my arms. While they swamped the guards in the confusion, we snuck down onto the tracks. We made it past the gates as they lowered."

Mateo cleared his throat. "Once we arrived here, I scanned her physiology to discover what was happening. The chemical was poisoning her at a fast rate. It attacked her capacity to heal. I had to act fast or lose her. They had yet to approve human trials for our genetic engineering project."

He eyed General Johnson. "I was trying to save her, so I cared nothing about approvals. It is better to ask forgiveness than permission."

Mateo looked at Sofia. "This laboratory is state-of-the art and equipped with everything that I needed. I told her my plan. She struggled to raise her hand, but caressed my cheek and asked me to do it. I kissed her on the forehead and started working."

He circled Jack another time. "The compound was killing her faster than I expected. I had to supercharge her ability to recover to counteract that. The process was painful. Physically for her and emotionally for me. After the procedure, she lay unconscious for weeks. One morning a kiss on the cheek woke me."

Mateo smiled at Sofia. "I gazed at your mama and saw her glowing. Did she pass while I slept and visit me as the angel she was? Andrea, however, was very alive. The glow was a byproduct of the process."

He strode up to the barrier and glowered at the General. They stared at each other in silence.

Mateo then walked to Sofia. "At that point, I'd saved your mother. I rescued mi Corazón from death. After that, I had a choice to make. Move on like nothing happened and come back to you? That was what I wanted most. Another option was to reunite with you and devote my time to creating a cure to fight this chemical with a team of scientist based on my research and procedure. I should have done that. When I considered the victims and what they endured during the incident, I knew I had to take more drastic steps."

He strolled toward General Johnson. "Why just make the remedy without stopping the ones responsible? Kill them, everyone that knows of what they've created, and destroy instructions on how to create it."

Sofia moved nearer to the barrier. "Papa, this isn't you."

Mateo peered into her eyes. "You don't know this version of me. I changed when you were born. You don't know the complete story of my life. Things from a past variation of me."

He paused. "I'm not proud of the events in my history, but this is something that thrills me."

General Johnson stared at him. "So, were you successful in your task?"

Mateo chuckled. "I was triumphant. We tracked down the individuals responsible with a little help. I never forgot that very conspicuous tattoo, which led us to the culprits. The United Terrorist Against America. The U.T.A.A. formed from different radical organizations joining to deter the U.C.A. from bullying everyone without repercussions. They had a cell in this city. You knew that though, correct?"

The General reddened with anger.

Mateo leered. "I tracked them down using information in your database."

General Johnson looked at the Colonel. "That's not possible. It's unfeasible to attain that info with no detection. Any unauthorized access sends an activity flag."

Mateo snickered. "It's cute that you assume you know everything. You are ignorant about much."

He paced. "When we got to their hideout, we copied data on the chemicals and wiped it from their servers. My team rounded up anybody they had not already killed during the assault. I had them brought here for their punishment. Death was not a good enough sentence. They had to suffer the way their victims did. Worse than the manner Andrea suffered."

Mateo delayed. "I injected them with an altered version of the pestilence they unleashed. Then their bodies were prepared for what was next. As they deteriorated, I worked. I'd already decided on their fates before we captured them. All their hired henchmen became the first Reapers. A fitting name as they took innocent lives. I supercharged their power to heal, as I did with my wife. Then I increased their strength. Their loss of eyesight was a tradeoff that was fine with me. They were to do my grunt work. The Reapers didn't need vision to continue being mindless monsters. So, they're no different from what they were. I modified their hunger, so that plasma is what they craved. Modified their teeth and saliva. While they feast, they also inject a mutagen into their prey. I made them blue for the sadness they've set free on Allegheny and those families who lost members. Those whose genetic makeup wasn't compatible died during the process."

He kneeled next to Jack Lincoln. "Then I experimented on their scientists and ramped up their vision. It was fitting, since they couldn't perceive the error of their ways. I considered making them smarter, but they became slaves to my thoughts. Hence the name Thinkers. They were the brains behind the atrocity and now they cannot think for themselves. I love the irony."

Mateo scoffed. "They were already weak men, so their physiology remained unchanged. I turned their skin red, to signify the bloodshed in their ledger."

General Johnson glared at him. "What about the purple ones?"

Mateo glanced at the General. "Purple what?"

General Johnson clenched his teeth. "A Reaper injected a downed Thinker and turned it purple. Why'd you engineer them to do that? There are many unknowns on how they'll change. You can't control that."

Mateo beamed. "I didn't plan that. Evolution found a way. I had to leave room for mutation. Everything evolves, or it dies. How they evolved was not what I thought, but it pleases me."

He arose. "The problem is we think we can command life. I did. Look at my field of study. The bombing taught me we cannot influence everything. I can't control what the Taken evolve into, but there are things I can manipulate. This, for instance."

The unit watched him.

Liam stared at him. "What are we supposed to be watching?"

Something knocked the group to the ground. James gripped his ears to halt the ringing.

He touched Robert on his left. "Are you okay?"

Robert nodded in response to his father. James peered to his right for Sofia. She was not there. He looked up and found her on the opposite side of the forcefield with her dad and a yellow Taken restraining her. James rotated and watched Liam and Isaac stirring, and General Johnson pushing himself off the ground.

James observed Colonel Brian. "Oh no."

The Colonel laid there choking on his own blood, holding his bloody abdomen. Isaac and the General crawled over to him. Brian cried out in pain, and the pair focused on Mateo. Their faces were red. Mateo met their anger with a smirk.

Chapter Fifteen

James grabbed his head. He observed Colonel Brian lying in a pool of blood. James, Liam, and Robert stood back to give the Colonel, Isaac, and General Johnson room.

Brian pulled the General and Isaac closer. "Stop him. Find... her."

Isaac and General Johnson both nodded. Brian's lips stopped moving. His face fell to the right. Colonel Brian was gone, his eyes fixed upon Mateo.

Tears ran down Isaac, the General's, and Liam's faces.

Anger replaced it as General Johnson and Isaac sprang to their feet and moved towards the forcefield.

Mateo smirked. "Meet the Hunters. These Taken were the leaders of the organization. The heads of the hydra. They're fast as cheetahs. Great for killing those responsible for the deaths via bombings, all the way to the top person who's accountable."

Sofia struggled against the creature's grip. "Colonel Brian was not to blame for the bombing last year papa. The terrorists were."

Mateo smiled. "I agree. The Colonel was blameless for the attack on Allegheny. The United Terrorists Against America handled that, and I made this cell pay for it. I plan on punishing the remaining members as well."

He walked to the barrier and stared at the General. "Tell them about Capital City."

General Johnson glared at him.

Mateo grinned. "Nothing to say? Okay, I guess I'll have to do it."

Isaac gritted his teeth. "Get to the damn point. The quicker this story is over, the faster I can kill you."

Liam looked at his father.

Mateo waved his finger. "I won't be dying here. Only the guilty will perish tonight."

General Johnson scowled at him. "Are you going to stand there and paint yourself innocent while your creatures have slaughtered thousands?"

Mateo shook his head. "I have not killed them, I've Taken them. We've evolved them. I'm not guiltless; I just won't be among the guilty and the dead."

Sofia continued to struggle. "How is he at fault? He's acted as nothing but heroic tonight. Brian helped keep me alive while your monsters were attacking innocent people."

Mateo set his hand on her shoulder. "Do you remember the Capital City bombing two years ago?"

Everyone except the General and Isaac nodded.

Mateo pointed at General Johnson. "I know you recall the bombings Oliver. Better than anybody."

The General focused on him.

Mateo turned to the rest of the group. "Anyway, let me come to the point. As I've learned, the government received word of an imminent threat on Capital City. They communicated with the United Middle East about collaborating to extract the radicals. The U.M.E. rebuffed them. The army's leadership tried to get sanctioned for an operation to infiltrate and eliminate the targets. During a secret hearing to discuss it, a senator involved opposed the mission because of the denial through the proper procedures. He feared if the U.M.E. discovered them, it would start World

War Four. The senator swayed the others to his side, putting an end to the campaign."

Mateo concentrated on General Johnson. "Or did he? The General here traveled with a small team to eliminate them without approval. They entered the facility and killed the terrorists. One was the brother of the U.T.A.A.'s leader."

Everybody glanced at General Johnson and then refocused on Mateo. "One terrorist wasn't dead and launched a missile from a boat in international waters before being killed. It headed straight for the Office of the President. A soldier hacked into the guidance system and gained control, but they couldn't disarm it. They guided the missile. There was not enough time or propellant remained to clear the city. The saboteurs rigged the missile to explode when the timer or rocket fuel expired. They steered it away from our head of state, but could not send it to the river. It crashed in Capital City."

Mateo extended his arm. "The General there created the best result from a dire situation. If it would crash anyway and murder blameless citizens, it should take out a prime target alongside those lives. They received intel as they departed for this mission of the U.T.A.A. boss's location inside Capital City. The place was under surveillance. They believed the U.T.A.A. planned another attack in case the first failed. General Johnson ordered that location targeted."

Mateo glanced at Brian. "He steered the bomb."

The unit peered at the deceased Colonel Brian. Then they stared at the General.

General Johnson gazed at the Colonel. "That man is a hero. Do not let him tell you otherwise. The continents would've been in a state of disarray had we not done what we did."

The General looked at the ground. "Yes, innocent people died. They were going to die, and nothing would stop that. I thought if we at least cut the head off the snake, the body would perish."

Mateo slowly clapped. "That was touching. The problem is you failed, didn't you? The leader didn't die in the explosion."

He paused for a second. "But his wife and his seven-year-old daughter did."

The group looked at General Johnson. Sofia closed her eyes.

Mateo eyed him. "You had no idea what you were facing. Your plan was to cut off the snake's head. You just upset the hydra."

He paced around Jack again. "After the death of his spouse, child, and brother, the U.T.A.A. ringleader disappeared. For a year, he plotted his revenge. A simple bombing wasn't enough now."

Mateo pointed to General Johnson. "He made it personal."

The General looked at him. "My squad did our job. We saved the President, which was our primary objective. Collateral damage sucks, but we had to make a call. There aren't always good and bad choices. Sometimes there's the awful choice and a worse option. We attempted to turn lemons into lemonade and were unsuccessful. It's a shame that his girl died, but so did other children. Other husbands and wives because of what the terrorists set in motion. Their faces wake me up, every night."

Mateo held up his hands. "Please don't be mistaken. The innocent children are the ones that I care about the most. The difference is that their parents didn't turn around and bomb cities with chemicals."

He adjusted his black lab coat and put his hands behind him. "Anyhow, you should give thanks to me."

General Johnson scoffed. "Why in the hell should I thank you? For unleashing pestilence on Allegheny? You'd be dead already if you weren't cowering beyond that barrier."

Mateo chuckled. "I'm no coward. First, this forcefield is strategy. A subject that you have shown multiple times that you do not comprehend. Second, my associates and I did something you didn't when we raided the organization's local headquarters. We caught the honcho of the U.T.A.A."

The General's cheeks boiled. "Did you have your friends kill him?"

Mateo sighed. "After the stories I told you, do you think that fits my style? Now General, you're not that dense. I suppose I will spell it out for you with a riddle. What's fast, yellow, and bloodied your fellow?"

Everybody glowered at the Hunter.

General Johnson aimed his gun at Mateo. "Get out here and take what's coming to you. Bring your pet too. It's on my list as well."

Mateo wagged his finger. "I refuse to do that for multiple reasons. First, they call me the world's greatest genetic engineer. Obviously, I am not stupid. Second, breathing is my favorite exercise. I'd like to continue doing that. Third, what's my motivation to do so? A quick death and a prolonged nap? Waterboarding and bamboo up my nails? I must decline that offer. Plus, another thing before this conversation ends."

Mateo looked toward the Hunter. Its mouth opened. The Hunter's lengthy tongue hung out over its teeth. It clawed at the throat of Jack Lincoln until blood was everywhere and his neck barely connected his head to his body. His lifeless face peered at the General. James covered Robert's eyes and turned him from the scene.

Liam alternated between raising and lowering his weapon, resigning to the fact that he couldn't prevent it. "Why did you execute him? Jack Lincoln was faultless in this!"

Mateo leaned forward. "How do you suppose they got into the United Middle East? He flew them in and posed them as his security team. His company has been a front for illegal weapons manufacturing overseas for years. How else would they secure guns in the U.M.E.?"

He bent down and held Jack's head up, pulling the neck up a bit. "General, did you know that he also sold to the U.T.A.A.? His sales to them included firearms, grenades, and rocket launchers."

Mateo delayed for a moment. "Also, he sold them missiles and bombs."

The General's jaw dropped.

Mateo peered at Liam. "So yes, he helped to secure The Warehouse with his monstrosity of a headquarters, and he aided the army in saving the commander-in-chief. But Jack was also responsible for many deaths internationally and domestically. He provided those bombs that detonated on the North Side. Mr. Lincoln only appeared innocent."

General Johnson withdrew a grenade. "I'm not listening to this anymore. We've already listened for too long. That yellow monster killed Brian and countless other people tonight. You must atone for your crimes. The only civilians that died by my hand resulted from something I didn't start. You are guiltier than I ever was. Your creatures infected the entire city."

Mateo put up his right hand. "I wouldn't do that if I were you."

The General gripped it tighter. "Give me one good reason not to do it."

Mateo raised two fingers. "You'll just kill yourselves when it bounces back at you. Plus, you don't want to attract them."

The garage doors lifted to reveal Reapers on the other side.

Sofia peered at her father. "My friends had zero to do with this. Please spare them."

Mateo pulled her closer. "We'll see where their loyalties lie soon enough."

He hauled her to a door accompanied by the Hunter.

As they exited, he turned. "Send him my best."

Mateo and Sofia left the area.

General Johnson surveyed the situation.

He peeked at Isaac. "I'll throw a grenade. It'll destroy them, but attract more. I'll need your help to move Brian to a HoverVan."

Isaac examined the mass of Reapers. "Aren't they a little close for that?"

The General held up his hand. "It's a Sonic Grenade. Its blast zone is very condensed but powerful."

Isaac nodded and grabbed the legs of Colonel Brian in preparation.

General Johnson glanced at Liam, James, and Robert. "Search for any opening or weakness. You won't have much time, so do it fast."

The three of them scanned for a solution. The General hurled it into the crowd of Reapers. Sonic force ripped the Taken apart. Limbs and blue blood flew in every direction. A chorus of pulse roars sounded in the distance. Isaac and General Johnson carried Colonel Brian into the HoverVan and placed him in the rear.

The General concentrated on James, Robert, and Liam. "Find anything yet?"

James aimed at the wall. "Liam, those metal boxes look like they're powering the barrier. You think I can overcharge them with the electric rods to break the forcefield?"

Liam shrugged. "I'm not sure, but it's the best idea we have."

James shot the containers with his Shock Rifle. The enclosures sparked.

Liam glimpsed at James as the Reapers approached. "Come on."

The General glanced at Isaac. "How close are they?"

Isaac focused on the entrance. "They're almost at the entrance."

James released more rounds into the boxes and the barrier disappeared. The garage door headed for the ground.

Liam turned. "Dad? What are you doing?"

Isaac stood there aiming his pistol. "Saving you. Catch him and hold him accountable for Brian. I'll hold them back."

Liam ran towards his father. "No. Come with us."

Isaac smiled. "I love you."

Liam reached for him. "Dad!"

Isaac hit the lifting mechanism with a gunshot. The gate shut before Liam arrived.

He pounded on the exit. "No!"

Outside, Isaac fired his pistol. "Come and get it you bastards."

They heard more pulsing roars and shots moving beyond the garage. The roaring faded as they passed.

Liam touched the garage door and his head fell. "No!"

Robert and James went to him. James grasped Liam's shoulders. "We have to finish the mission. If we are successful, we'll save millions of lives. Isn't that why he bought us a chance?"

Liam collected himself. "Yeah. Let's capture this son of a bitch."

They turned and General Johnson was nowhere in sight. James, Liam, and Robert approached the van and opened the door. Colonel Brian's body was there, the General wasn't.

James looked at Liam. "Think he chased after Mateo?"

Liam nodded. "We need to get there ASAP. This whole situation stinks. The good guys are turning out to be anti-heroes."

Robert looked at them. "What do we do now?"

James eyed the way Mateo and Sofia exited. "We save her and finish this. For Colonel Brian."

Liam seized his Sonic Shotgun with both hands. "Yeah, let's catch him."

They moved to the door. James opened it and Liam took the lead. They stepped onto the white tile floor and traveled down a long dark hallway until they came to a deactivated GravLift.

James looked at Liam. "How do we turn it on?"

The lift turned on and a quarantine fog activated in front of it.

Liam shook his head. "He's bringing us to him. That's the biggest mistake he has made all night."

Chapter Sixteen

J ames, Robert, and Liam exited the GravLift into a room with a white tile floor and walls. The dark area was lit only by three giant fluid filled tanks with green lights illuminating them. A desk and chair sat in the middle of the space. A trio of HoloPads laid on top of it.

Robert approached a tank. "Dad, these have Taken in them."

James and Liam inspected the other two containers near that wall.

He turned to Liam. "They look similar but different from The Taken we've fought so far. Are these rejects?"

Liam nodded. "Must be. We would remember seeing these on the streets."

They made their way to the desk. Each of them grabbed a HoloPad and unlocked it.

Robert pointed to his pad. "This one only has a file. It says here that these were the first attempts at making Taken."

James nodded. "That makes sense. They appear to be Reapers, but something's... weird."

Liam showed the folder on his. "My HoloPad has three files. Mateo had personnel documents on Jack Lincoln, Colonel Brian, and General Johnson. He knew everything about them before tonight. There are notes all over these files. The General has assassinated people in his career, completed covert ops and... whoa."

James looked toward Liam. "What is it?"

Liam displayed the information for him. "He did something redaction worthy to gain funding for his base. General Johnson seems to be worse than we feared."

James glanced at Liam. "Do you think he was aware of more than he shows?"

Liam peered at him. "I'm willing to believe that he and Mateo are in this together. Nothing is as it looks with this guy."

James finished poring over the information on his HoloPad. He put his hand on his helmet.

Liam pivoted to him. "What is it?"

James directed them to a name in the file. "Look who owns this building."

Liam read the identity. "Oh, come on."

Robert strolled over and examined the name. "Really? This day is the worst."

Both of Liam's hands were on his head. "So, these were the first tries at producing Reapers. General Johnson is a bad boy, and you can't trust anybody. The question is why did Mateo leave these HoloPads? Do you suppose it's an attempt to persuade us he's the good guy in this?"

James peeped at him. "It sure seems like that's his aim. But why would he try to convince us?"

Liam directed him to General Johnson's record. "So that we turn against him."

James examined it. "Even if he's the best of the worst, he needs to answer for his crimes and fix this. There has to be a cure."

Liam nodded. "There must be. General Johnson has a major lead for certain. Who knows what he'll do if we don't get there soon? Let's go."

They left the chamber and headed down a bright hallway. Shiny white walls complimented the white tile flooring. A white automatic door at the terminus slid open when they approached. They entered a massive area with tiling and walls that matched the hallway's esthetic. The ShadeGlass windows were all blacked out. Tables full of scientific equipment and standalone machines were on both sides of a hospital bed. A metal table sat at the room's heart. General Johnson was on his knees being detained by two purple Evolved Thinkers.

Mateo waved them closer. "The remarkable thing about the Evolved Thinkers is that they're smart enough to find their direction home. Plenty clever to trap a man, with adequate strength to subdue him."

He studied them for a second. "I wasn't sure if you would make it past your test. How did you like the guided tour? The General rushed beyond it."

They walked towards Mateo and the Hunter restraining Sofia.

James peered at Mateo. "The lesson was revelatory. What were you trying to show us?"

Mateo smiled. "With the Reapers, I wanted to show you how far I've come from the first unfortunate attempts. I might've changed a few things and created an easier process for myself, but I had a goal in mind. Stopping wasn't an option until they were perfect. Every design choice was intentional. Each decision I've made since the bombing leading to this point was deliberate. I had enough involuntary volunteers to try repeatedly."

Mateo turned to Sofia. "The occurrence that wasn't intentional, but a welcomed surprise, is my daughter being brought to me. She says I have you to thank for it. My quarrel isn't with you, so let me extend my deepest gratitude."

James and Robert watched him. Liam rested his palm on his holstered gun.

Mateo clapped. "How did you enjoy my expose? Weren't those facts intriguing?"

Liam swiveled to General Johnson. "Yeah, there sure was a lot of information about you and Mr. White I never would've assumed. It seems you've been a very wayward individual. When I first saw your base, it impressed me. Brand new and state-of-the-art everything. I saw what you did to get it."

The General tried to break free from the purple Taken. "You know nothing Liam Smith. Have you ever been on a battlefield? Had to save the President, or protect millions of citizens? Until you have, do not lecture me on what I've done or how I got my funding. I'll be damned if I am going to let you tell me that my means didn't justify the ends. Everything I do is to defend civilians."

Mateo raised his hand in objection. "Ignore that last line. That was a lie too. Why not reveal your work with Mr. White?"

The General's eyes narrowed, and his face flushed with rage. He stayed silent.

Mateo squatted. "What's the matter? Don't want them to know?"

General Johnson stared at him.

Mateo waved both hands. "No worries. I love storytelling."

He examined James, Liam, and Robert. "Did you notice anything when you were on The Agency's impressive underground train?"

Liam glanced at James. "Yeah, we noticed the HoverTrain had cargo and passenger cars."

James nodded. "I also saw yellow residue by the tracks."

Mateo applauded. "You are very observant. The freight attachments were used to transport samples to The Agency. That yellow sediment was from an accident where a container dropped. Ask him why they've been transporting Remnant to their scientists."

Liam stared at General Johnson. "Answer the question."

The General looked at Liam top to bottom. "Who the hell are you to tell me what to do?"

Liam squatted. "The cop that doesn't care what motivations you or Mr. White have. My motivation is to fix this situation. That kid lost his mother, and my father risked his life to buy us time. So quit being an ass and answer me."

General Johnson glared at him. Liam turned to Mateo.

Mateo leered at the General. "They intended to replicate it for use against their enemies. Even though it violates the International Laws of War."

Everyone eyed General Johnson.

Liam peered at Mateo. "What did you steal from the crates?"

Mateo positioned his arms behind him. "Power. Or rather, the ability to exert it by taking it away. One box contained experimental Electro Magnetic Pulse bombs. I used those to cripple the city. We did not steal the contents of the other container. I took back what was mine."

He observed the General. "We were working with Mr. White on a veritable fountain of youth. I was about to solve the last hurdle before the attack. As a contractor, what I made didn't belong to me. I couldn't copy it or send it to myself. After the attack, I needed to access the research to help save my wife. When I accessed it, Mr. White saw my activity. He sees all."

General Johnson struggled to free himself. "You are a liar. Mr. White would have told me if he knew you were alive."

Mateo went over and towered over the subdued soldier. "Has there been anything he hasn't communicated to you recently?"

The General was silent.

Mateo leaned closer. "Do not think this situation is any different. If someone omits details once, they'll do it again. Or they already had."

He walked back. "Mr. White stopped by to discover what was happening. He realized what I'd done before he showed up. I had been working on my Eternal Youth formula and a formula for human enhancement since I became a genetic engineer. Longevity and advancement should have been my legacy."

Mateo paused for a moment. "Andrea's survival was on the line. I used that work as a basis for the mutation protocol. This variation of the formula targeted areas instead of the whole. I tweaked the human enhancement research by adding elements of the Fountain formula. Including Remnant proved... fruitful. The Evolution formula was born. Once I showed him my progress with the research, it intrigued Mr. White. I informed him of my plans, and he loaned me men to achieve those goals."

James waved his arm. "Mr. White lent you personnel to capture the terrorists?"

Mateo aimed a finger at him. "Precisely. He also supplied me with abundant samples of Remnant to create as many Taken as I desired."

Sofia stared at her father.

Mateo smirked. "We thought it very serendipitous that I'd modified their poison and turned them into the monsters they were. In exchange, I would manufacture a version of Evolution without the mutations. That would be my greatest achievement. Taken were a temporary means to an end. Knowing how ruthless Mr. White is, I was keeping them around until after delivery."

He peered at Sofia. "After the trade, the Taken were supposed to be destroyed, and we'd come for you."

The Evolved Thinkers roared and loosened their grip on General Johnson. Mateo gave the creatures a death stare. They restored their hold.

Mateo placed his arms behind him. "Mr. White wished to put together a team of super agents to change the world. He wanted to rid the planet of terrorists and murderers. Obviously, I was in favor of that. After we finished handing out judgment to the guilty, I developed the formulas for Mr. White. It took until yesterday, but Andrea and I did it. We met with his lead scientist and a few of Mr. White's operatives at The Warehouse at midnight. Andrea and I brought along this Hunter, a Thinker, and multiple Reapers. They perceived it as a sign of aggression. I calmed things down, and we continued with the delivery. We presented them with the vials of the completed compounds. Mr. White's hologram showed up to the head agent through DirectLink. I could not hear their conversation. They reached for their weapons."

He shook his head. "I expected it, but I was still disappointed. Before he or any of his men pointed them, the Hunter standing with me attacked. As did the two Hunters flanking them, they never knew were there."

Mateo looked at Sofia. "I had just saved her and hadn't planned on losing her twice. We helped ourselves to the E.M.P. bombs as compensation for that insult. I figured if we cheated the grim reaper, we should loot from his sender. The goal of elevating humanity is why I was happy to collaborate with him. I did not plan to release The Taken on the world. The plans were to purge them."

The purple Taken growled and relaxed their grips again.

Mateo continued. "After the attempt on our lives, I added Mr. White to my list of targets. Digging deeper into him and his associates, I realized his influence was everywhere in Allegheny. I must cleanse this city to get rid of him and his disciples."

He kneeled in front of General Johnson. "Had he not attempted to kill us, I wouldn't have unleashed The Taken. I would've followed protocol.

We would have found our daughter and left Allegheny. Everything that has happened is Mr. White's fault."

James eyeballed him. "You can't purge the city at your discretion. Innocents are dying out there. People with no idea Mr. White exists. How are their deaths justified?"

Mateo gazed at the Hunter. "When you have the power I do, you decide who is innocent or not."

The Hunter's eyes darted left to right before it sprang high into the air headed at James.

Sofia seized her Acid Pistol and aimed it at her dad. "No!"

Robert stepped past his father to protect him. "No!"

The yellow Taken was descending onto them. James rotated Robert around and braced himself.

'*I can't die this way.*' he thought.

Mateo held out his hand. The Hunter landed and loomed over James with its claws in the air.

It turned to the right and bared its teeth at Liam, who had his firearm aimed at Mateo.

Mateo wiggled his finger. "Don't be silly. If either of you pull the trigger, all of you perish."

Liam tightened his hold on the pistol. "So will you."

Mateo motioned, then the Hunter returned to its post beside him. James opened his eyes. He turned and glared at Mateo. Sofia gave a wide berth while still aiming at her father and approached Liam, James, & Robert.

James eyed Mateo. "Why haven't you killed us yet?"

Mateo glanced at Sofia. "You protected my daughter through all this madness, and somehow you ended up here. Since you brought her to me, I'll repay you by not killing you, your friend, and your son. Three souls for a single life is more than a fair trade I believe."

Liam shrugged his shoulders. "So, what happens after you clean up Allegheny? What next? Who lives here? Who rebuilds what you destroyed? What will happen with the Taken that were created?"

Mateo smiled. "We live here. All my Taken, and those who decide to join us on our quest to purge Earth. That is who will rebuild this city."

Liam palmed his face. "You've graduated from Allegheny to the world? That's a gigantic leap. Why the planet? You cannot eliminate everyone."

Mateo marched by them to the Evolved Thinkers and grabbed one creature's outside shoulder. "What you see as death, I regard as culling and evolving. Anyone who attacks The Taken is fighting adaptation. The individuals who embrace it choose to evolve into something greater than themselves. Better than they even dreamed of being. If they're unsuccessful at combatting change, then they perish. No room for descension. If they can kill my creations, they deserve to survive... for the moment. They will volunteer and become Taken or die resisting the inevitable. So now I ask you, do you wish to join me? Or will you be taken?"

James grasped his Shock Rifle. "Your monsters murdered my child's mom and my neighbors. I would never follow you."

Robert clutched his weapon.

General Johnson smirked. "You know my choice."

Liam grabbed his Sonic Shotgun and shook his head. "I'd rather flatline trying to bring you in or stop you. My father gambled himself for that purpose. I won't betray that sacrifice. So, you're gonna treat the folks you've infected, or I'm going to fire on you and your freaks."

Mateo bellowed. "There's no cure for evolution. What is will be. There is no moving backward, only forward."

He sneered. "It's a shame. You are throwing your futures away over ideals that were branded into you. Don't tell me you think humans aren't monstrous."

James eyed him. "People have been and can be evil. They also could be selfless and loyal. Purging a city for the mistakes of a few makes you a bigger monster than them and The Taken you produced. Someone advised me doing the right thing is the only thing. Allying with you is the wrong pick."

Mateo sucked his teeth. "Such a pity. I need to break my daughter's heart by having her friends killed."

Liam shook his head. "Not before we off you."

James, Liam, and Robert all raised their guns. All the Taken in the vicinity pulse roared.

Sofia stepped in between them and held up her hand. "Stop! Nobody is hurting anybody. You won't touch my dad."

She turned to Mateo. "You will not harm my friends."

Liam implied she should step to her right with the Sonic Shotgun. "Move aside. We have a mission to do because your father is a lunatic. Innocent people need treatment. If force is the only way, then so be it. It's not personal."

Sofia glared at him. "It would be to me."

General Johnson resisted against his captors. "Do it Liam. Think of your dad and Colonel Brian. James and Robert, remember Candace."

Robert's grasp tightened on the trigger.

James jumped in front of him. "Do not shoot. You may hit Sofia."

Robert looked around his father. "Move Sofia. Your dad's monsters killed my mom. He doesn't get to just leave unpunished and keep killing."

Sofia gazed at James. "Make them stop. Please."

He glanced at her. "Think about what happened to Lydia."

Mateo gripped her shoulder. "Pay no attention to them. I shall prove myself correct in the end."

She snatched her arm away and turned to her dad. "You have hurt everyone here papa, including me. I want to defend you because you're my father, but it's not possible. This isn't how you and mama raised me."

She walked to James.

Mateo chuckled. "That's a turn of events. Well, I guess we'll have to go through you too."

A massive force burst through the area, knocking down everything and everyone.

A voice rode the power. "Enough!"

In strode a person whose white luminescence was almost blinding. The figure held out their hand and pulled all the weapons towards it. They crushed their hands together and all the guns fell to the floor as an enormous ball of metal.

She headed to Sofia. "I'm so disappointed in you."

Sofia shielded her eyes. "Mama?"

Chapter Seventeen

S ofia got up off the white tile floor. "Mama, is that you?"

Andrea Hernandez was fifty-two years old.

Her light tan skin had a dazzling white luminescence.

Andrea's eyes were blue green.

She stood five feet five inches tall, had a slim-thick physique with short curly black hair.

Andrea stood there in a white lab coat with an orange blouse and blue jeans. She smiled at her daughter. Sofia ran to her. They hugged each other and cried.

Andrea held Sofia's face as she stared at her. "Hola mi Princesa. I have missed you so. We didn't know if we'd ever see you again after everything that happened last year."

Sofia pointed to her dad, who sat against the blacked out ShadeGlass. "You have to stop papa. He's killing innocent people with his Taken."

Andrea peered at her. "I'll do no such thing. Your father is justified in doing what he has. Look at all we lost because of the monsters that bombed Capital City. The same terrorists attacked Allegheny. They almost killed me. The killers caused themselves to be made into beasts. Then our own betrayed us after we helped bring the radicals to justice. There's no difference between governments and terrorists. We just tolerate one group's terrorism and despise the other."

Sofia shook her head. "No mama. You dealing with the extremists, I can accept. Going after the government officials who tried to kill you, I could even understand that. I won't stand by while the people that raised me to be a loving person are killing innocent citizens. Anger is a choice that kills us from the inside. Choose forgiveness and life, or anger and death. You taught me that."

Mateo held out his hand. "Naivety guided our thoughts then. We believed we left our past behind us. Those actions did not define us. They were what we had to do. We thought we'd raise you to be better than us. At least we succeeded in that."

He motioned towards Sofia. "I tried to talk to her. She doesn't understand."

Andrea held up her palm, and Mateo quieted.

She turned to Sofia. "We taught you those things because we had to do unspeakable stuff to survive as youths. Your father and I departed Colombia and came to this continent for a better life. Then we had you. We vowed you would be the best of our family. He and I also swore that we would change the Earth for the better. That world attempted to slay us. We are fighting for our right to live. Our intentions chilled with our betrayal. At its core, this government's no improvement over the one we fled."

Sofia stepped away from Andrea. "Whatever you did in your youth does not define who you are. You created a greater lifestyle and come to be the parents that I love. Scientists around the globe revere you for your efforts. We could be the greatest in the world. You, papa, and I. Not only me. Reverting to who you were is a choice. It's not a mandate or an unavoidable outcome."

Sofia stepped closer to Andrea and grabbed her hands. "Helping the planet was your purpose. Will you die trying to kill the world you intended to improve?"

Andrea opened her mouth, but no words escaped. She fired out her left hand and closed it. Menace spread on her visage. She looked left and sucked her teeth.

Andrea waved her right index finger. "I believed you were smarter than that Oliver."

The General crept within arm's reach of Andrea before she stopped him psychokinetically. A green tinted blade was in his right fist.

Andrea controlled his hand and clasped tighter. "Drop the poison coated knife or I crush the bones in your hand into dust."

General Johnson dropped the dagger but caught it with his left and thrust it at her. Andrea's right hand clenched, and she commanded his left hand as well. She closed her right hand. That broke his left hand. He gritted his teeth and released the weapon. With a yell, she pushed both arms towards the General, throwing him through the air.

He bounced off the white wall with a thud before falling to the floor. General Johnson laid there motionless. Sofia backed away. Andrea spun and held out her right palm. Sofia froze.

She struggled to free herself. "Let me go. You are not the mom I knew. Now you are something different. I won't be part of this."

Andrea pulled Sofia to her. "Family is everything. Even if you think we're wrong, you stick by us no matter what."

Sofia looked at her mother. "If that's true, why didn't you want me over revenge?"

Andrea gazed at her.

Sofia's eyes watered. "Please end this. Wrong is wrong. This is crazy."

Andrea's left hand shot out. "Come along, or I kill your boyfriend."

James grasped at his neck. Robert watched his dad struggle to breathe.

He glared at Andrea. "Stop hurting my dad!"

Liam sprinted toward her with his fist balled. "Release him!"

She dropped Sofia and swatted at him with her right hand. Andrea knocked him backward several yards onto his back. James' eyes met with Sofia's. His eyelids fluttered.

She turned to her mother. "Alright! Just don't hurt them."

Andrea released her psychokinetic grip on James' neck. Robert hugged him as he gasped for breath.

She yanked Sofia close to her. "Do as I say, and things will be okay."

Andrea extended a finger. "Do not disobey me again."

Sofia nodded.

Andrea smiled. "Much better."

She gazed at Mateo. "Let's go. That should be enough time."

He directed Sofia to grab a briefcase.

Mateo spun to the group. "You three helped my child tonight. I will return the favor. My Taken won't harm you for the next twenty-four hours. After that, you are on your own. Do not follow us or we'll cancel that deal. I suggest you get far away from this city, but don't grow too comfortable. We will reach wherever you end up sooner than you think."

He turned and ushered Sofia toward the door. She peered back at James as Mateo shoved her through the exit. He rotated and nodded at them. The Hunter and Evolved Thinkers followed them out. They heard stirring to their left. James, Liam, and Robert ran over to find General Johnson. His left hand hung there as he held it up by his wrist.

Liam scratched his helmet. "How are you still alive?"

The General maneuvered to one knee. "It's going to take more than a glowing woman and crushed bones to break me."

Liam shook his head.

General Johnson raised to his feet. "There's a job to do. Whatever happens, it needs to be accomplished somehow."

Liam eyed James. "What are you thinking?"

James pointed towards the door. "We save Sofia and get her parents."

General Johnson looked at him. "For all we know, she's been in on this the whole time. Maybe it's an act. We need to apprehend them all."

James walked up to the General. "Sofia's a part of it as much as I am. She is innocent and you know it. You're more responsible for this than she is."

General Johnson stared at him. Gunfire came from the rooftop. Liam and James exchanged a look, then they and Robert moved from the room. The General trailed behind them. James, Robert, and Liam ran up the stairs until they reached the roof. As they opened the door, Mateo, Andrea, and Sofia were on the pathway straight ahead. They walked towards a HoverCopter. The pilot waved them on. Giant cooling vents and exhausts lined the path.

Two spotlights activated. Bullets flew at Mateo, Sofia, and Andrea. They lunged left for cover. The pilot hopped in the chopper. James, Robert, and Liam grabbed shelter on their left. When the shots ended, James peeked around the left edge. Two HoverCopters were in the sky. Sofia, her father, and her mom took cover two rows of vents in front of them. Their Taken escorts and scouts lay riddled with bullet holes in the walkway to their aircraft. Sofia locked eyes with him while her parents looked at their attackers. She raised her arms to chest level and glanced at the ground. James nodded.

Mateo glanced at Andrea. "How are we gonna deal with two HoverCopters?"

She studied them in the air. "I got this."

Andrea turned to exit cover, and he seized her arm. "Are you sure?"

She smiled and stepped onto the path. The choppers aimed their spotlights at her.

One male pilot spoke through a speaker on his vehicle. "Mateo and Andrea Hernandez, surrender now."

Andrea shook her head.

The female pilot interjected. "If you do not come willingly, we must use force."

She grinned. "I choose option two."

Andrea threw out both of her hands in the HoverCopters' direction and shut them. She straightened both arms out to her sides, and both aircraft whirled as she moved them to each side. Andrea clapped her palms together, and both HoverCopters spun at each other until they crashed, exploded, and fell to the ground.

A third chopper arrived and fired at her. She stretched her hands forward and created a bright wall of white light. Everywhere bullets struck the energy shield, the brightness intensified. Andrea let out a scream. The HoverCopter ceased fire. She flung both hands towards it. All the ammo she'd stopped now sped up at the chopper along with the power in sphere form. The bullets ripped through the front of it, killing the occupants. Once the orb hit the chopper, it detonated, and the fiery frame plummeted to the pavement.

James watched the third HoverCopter fall. '*How are we supposed to stop her?*' he thought.

Andrea looked at her family.

Her husband was gleeful. Sofia had a look of terror.

Mateo jumped to his feet. "Shall we move to the HoverCopter and leave this place?"

Andrea led while he pulled Sofia by the hand. The group crept to where they were.

James marched onto the pathway. "Free her."

Andrea and Mateo whirled round to face him.

Mateo chuckled. "I believe I was very generous in giving you a twenty-four-hour head start. If you insist on dying, I can accommodate that."

James looked at him. "Nobody is killing anyone. We have no weapons, so we are not a threat to hurt you. Release Sofia, then we'll leave."

Mateo laughed. "We have already won. Just accept it. Why would we give her to you?"

James gazed at Sofia. "Look at her. She doesn't want to go with you. Sofia didn't decide to be involved in this."

Andrea observed her.

Tears ran down Sofia's face. "Let me go, please."

Andrea glared at James. "She is our only child. Nothing can replace that."

He elevated a briefcase and placed it on his chest. "How about his life's work? Do you have more of this?"

Andrea scoffed. "That doesn't equal Sofia."

James walked to the edge of the building and stepped onto the ledge.

He hugged the briefcase. "Are you certain? I'll throw it over the side, and you take Sofia. Or you save your greatest work, Mateo, and let her walk. She'll be happier for whatever amount of time we have remaining before your plague kills humanity. Don't waste all your blood, sweat, and tears. If she tries to grab me, that may damage the contents of the case. What's it gonna be?"

Mateo stared at Andrea.

She glowered at him. "You can't be serious. We discussed this day for twelve months! After we avenged our betrayal, we would reunite with Sofia. We waited for a year. I waited!"

Mateo nodded his head. "It's not over yet. We need the Evolution formula. That is all we have of it. We cannot afford to lose it."

He eyed Sofia. "Go. You better hope you're making the correct choice."

She faced her mother. Andrea teared up as she looked her in the eye. Fire replaced the tears when she eyeballed Mateo. Sofia strode over to James. Andrea stared at him. Once Sofia reached them, he placed the briefcase on the ground. Andrea lifted the case to her.

Mateo examined the squad. "One day is all you get. That goes for you too, Sofia. You've chosen your side. Deal with the fallout of that."

He and Andrea entered their HoverCopter and rose skyward. Sofia turned to James. She clenched him in her arms and then kissed him. He clutched her tight.

Sofia loosened her grip and stared at James. "Thank you for risking your life to help me. I left the briefcase there to use as a bargaining chip later, maybe. How did you know they would swap me for the case?"

James grabbed her hand. "The way your dad talked about this formula. Children are most parent's life work. Some people offer their whole life to their kids. Others won't give any of it. His focus shifted to the Taken and super agents after the bombing. I wasn't sure if your mom would trade you to get the case, but I thought your father might."

Sofia shook her head. "My mother is not happy right now. It sucks that they got away with all they've done. They're not who they were before the attack."

Liam placed his hand on her shoulder. "You've chosen the right side. Your parents will answer for what they have unleashed. We must locate them and bring them in before Mr. White does. He might not be non-lethal."

Sofia scanned his expression. "What about your father?"

Liam sighed. "I don't know if he's alive or dead, but we must continue the mission. We owe him that much."

As Mateo and Andrea flew forth, an ear-piercing scream filled the atmosphere.

The group covered their ears.

James observed the copter. '*Was that Andrea?*' he thought.

The chopper pulled to a hover. It rotated until it faced their direction.

Liam pointed. "That's not good."

A rocket soared past the HoverCopter's left window from street level. Liam dashed right to the boundary of the roof.

He peered over the edge. "It's General Johnson. He's down there with two agents."

James, Sofia, and Robert rushed to see. The General was standing between two of the crashed copters. He held the rocket launcher on his right shoulder while an agent reloaded it. General Johnson aimed and launched another missile.

Sofia stretched her arm out. "No!"

This one was on target. It paused at the HoverCopter's door.

Andrea had both hands up to halt it with an energy shield.

She twisted her hands, and the projectile rotated. The General and the two men ran.

As she twirled it, a new chopper shot at them. The projectile flew from her control when she ducked to avoid the shots. It hit feet to the left of the operatives and General Johnson, tossing them in different directions. The bullets struck their tail rotor. It smoked as they struggled to keep altitude.

Sofia covered her mouth. "No. No, no, no."

Andrea swatted her palm to the right, and she knocked the other chopper into a building. It smoked as it fell to the concrete. Mateo and Andrea's aircraft turned south and disappeared into the night sky as it lost elevation. They raced down the steps, through the labs, to the GravLift, and descended to street level. The group exited an opened garage to the boulevard.

James searched skyward to the left. "The smoke leads south."

He investigated the street. "It looks like The Taken have dispersed."

They proceeded to the corner and looked left. Four crashed HoverCopters burned on the right side of the structure. They walked past the point of impact of the rocket. The two agents laid there still.

James looked left. "Quick, over here."

They approached the General and found him lying there, missing his left leg and left arm. Liam put his fingers on his neck.

He addressed the group. "I can't detect a pulse."

They glanced at each other. The sound of HoverCopters in the distance broke the silence.

Liam stared at everyone. "Let's get out of Mr. White's building before his friends arrive. I don't think he'll welcome us this time."

They reentered the garage, went to the HoverVan, and entered. Liam took the wheel and started the vehicle. Robert sat next to him. James and Sofia huddled in the rear.

She examined the back of the van. "Colonel Brian's body is gone."

Everyone turned.

James looked at Liam. "Let's go."

He reversed before exiting to the right.

Liam looked at James. "I knew something was wrong with Mr. White from the jump. Hand me your communicators."

He tossed them out the window as they drove. Watching on the other end of the feed, Mr. White sipped his drink.

He put down his glass. "Smart kid."

Chapter Eighteen

Smoke filled the air in the dark office. The only illumination came from a hologram that showed the casualty projections. Mr. White sat puffing a cigar at his black wood desk. An agent peered through the window. He breathed deep and knocked at the open doorway.

Mr. White puffed the Havana once more and exhaled the smoke. "Enter."

The operative walked in and shut the door.

Mr. White held his cigar. "Give me the full report."

The agent cleared his throat. "Agents used the same route General Johnson's group traveled to go to Hernandez Labs after they finished their task. When the agents arrived, they found Colonel Brian's body in a van. They transported his remains here. Agents worked their way up the steps and signaled the General, who stayed as the civilians pursued the targets. Andrea Hernandez shattered his left hand. Mateo Hernandez wiped almost everything from the cloud. We couldn't retrieve the file you wanted, but we recovered info on something called Project X. It may interest you. I've added it to your database."

Mr. White stared at the operative. "What about the targets?"

The agent coughed. "Andrea Hernandez destroyed all four HoverCopters. Two of the men escorted General Johnson to the street, where he demanded they give him a rocket launcher. Mrs. Hernandez killed them in the ensuing battle and the General lost his left arm and left leg in an explosion. At that point, I pulled the remaining team out."

Mr. White put the Havana up to his lips and huffed once again. "Your instructions were to capture Andrea, bring me Mateo, and what he owes me."

The operative swallowed. "Sir, we already lost all the HoverCopters and eleven people. We didn't gain the formula, or apprehend Mrs. Hernandez, but you'll be very interested in Project X."

Mr. White stared at him. "I did not task you with bringing me information on this plan. Your goal was to deliver me the Evolution formula, or the research. You brought me neither."

The agent stood tall. "I won't fail you a second time, sir."

Mr. White smiled at him. "I know."

The operative turned to leave. Mr. White snapped his fingers. The agent collapsed to the floor. Mr. White read the file on his HoloPad.

He peered over the desk at the dead operative. "I should've listened to him. Huh."

Mr. White buzzed his assistant. "Send in the cleaners."

The door opened and two people came into the dim office. The younger man hesitated while the older one moved inside as usual. They lifted the body.

Before they exited, Mr. White raised his hand, and they froze. "Make sure he has a nice ceremony. Be certain to compensate his family for his excellent work."

Mr. White's aide shut the door. He took an additional drag. Mr. White gasped and dropped the cigar into the ashtray. He grabbed his skull and screamed.

The assistant knocked. "Are you alright?"

Mr. White held out his hand. "Yes! Do not come in here!"

He leaned over in his seat and ran his hands through his hair as the pain lessened. "Damn side effects."

Mr. White rose, straightened his necktie, and seized his jacket off his black wood chair. He reached for the door and breathed deeply before he exited.

Mr. White looked at his aide. "Tell her I need to HoloConference with her in fifteen minutes."

The assistant opened his communicator. Mr. White walked into the main hallway. Through the glass double doors ahead, he saw scientists working frantically. Mr. White went right and reached an area off the corridor. He proceeded between two armed guards. The man at the desk held up two fingers. Mr. White entered room number two. He closed the door, removed his suit jacket, and placed it on the steel chair. Mr. White loosened his tie and took a seat at the metal desk. He grabbed a cigar, a cutter, and an instant flame from the inner pocket. Mr. White cut the Havana, lit it, and puffed several times to get it going before exhaling.

He glimpsed across the table. "How are you doing?"

His guest didn't respond.

Mr. White pointed to his brain. "Did you create your digital psyche and have it evaluated?"

His visitor gave a thumbs up.

Mr. White took another draw. "Losing people is hard, but we honor them by remembering to live and achieve. I imagine coming here was difficult for you, considering the totality, but you made the correct choice."

He leaned back. "It doesn't feel good in your gut? I understand. Sometimes we must do what's best, if it's perceived like that or not. Even by our own morals. That's our duty to humanity. You trusted your instincts, do not second guess that. In the end, they will view you as justified. Anyone who'd criticize you now, would acknowledge so then."

The person leaned forward. "I'm still not positive if I should trust you. My mind thinks this choice is better, my heart says otherwise. There's only one thing that I ask of you."

Mr. White matched his guest's posture. "What's that?"

The guest cleared their throat. "No harm can come to my child. If something happens, I'll guarantee you pay."

Mr. White laughed. He inhaled his cigar another time.

Mr. White exhaled with a smile. "Do I look like someone you threaten? I'm the guy you apologize to for looking at too long. The man that you move from your neighborhood when you see me walking towards you. You don't realize why; you just do it because of the feeling you have. I'm a person you send to kill the guy you hired to murder the monster. The only man I fear is God. That being said, let's not start this partnership on a poor foot. This is not how I prefer to conduct business. Let's be friends and do major things together."

The visitor nodded. They both rose.

Mr. White looked at them. "Take a walk with me."

He pushed the door, and they departed. They journeyed down the hallway towards The Lab.

Mr. White patted their back. "I promise, nothing shall happen to Liam."

Isaac glanced at him. "Okay. I wasn't trying to threaten you. As a father, I worry and protect."

Mr. White eyed him. "I forgive you this once, but never talk to me like that again. Individuals have died for much less."

Isaac peered at him. "I'm just happy your squad got there when they did. If they arrived a minute later, the Reapers would've slaughtered me."

Mr. White glanced at him. "I'm glad they did as well. It's unfortunate they did not arrive there in time to prevent the attack on Colonel Brian."

He paused. "You grew up together?"

Isaac frowned. "Yeah, in the old neighborhood. We've been friends since then."

He hesitated. "There's something that's eating at me. If you sent another team, why not send them with our group?"

Mr. White inspected him. "They were handling other business for me that was urgent, and unavoidable."

Isaac stopped in his tracks. "What was more vital than The Taken outbreak? I mean, we're attempting to stop the most dangerous pandemic in history."

Mr. White chuckled at him. "You'll understand in a moment. Since you've joined my organization after all of Brian's attempts, you're going to see what we do here."

Isaac scratched his head. "What do we do here? The Agency's purpose. Who do we answer to?"

Mr. White smirked. "Lots of things happen here. We formed the Agency for moments like this. Our goal is to defend the United Continents of America at all costs, against all threats. As of tonight, we don't report to anyone. Everyone in the government works for me."

He extended his arm. They walked into the clinic. Mr. White and Isaac arrived at a room with onlookers watching through the window. A scientist noticed Mr. White coming. He hit a coworker who turned. All the researchers cleared a path as he and Isaac entered. Two hospital beds rested in the center. Doctors and scientists surrounded the second. Isaac halted. His jaw dropped.

He dashed to the first bed. "Brian?"

Colonel Brian sat there with a smile at the sight of Isaac. "Hey buddy."

They hugged. Isaac laughed.

He stared at Brian. "I thought you were dead."

Colonel Brian nodded. "I was. Mr. White's scientists and doctors revived me."

Isaac spun around. "How did you do it?"

Mr. White grinned. "The procedure is very complicated, and expensive to do. Only one other person has undergone it. When you can save your most important people, you do so."

Brian laughed. "Most important, huh? I'm flattered."

They exchanged smiles.

Colonel Brian glanced at Isaac. "Where's Liam?"

Isaac glanced at Mr. White. "He's alive, but I have no clue where he is."

Brian clutched Isaac's shoulder. "Don't worry about him. He will take care of himself and his friends. Liam will be fine."

Isaac smiled. "You're right. Just fatherly worries."

Colonel Brian frowned. "Yeah. I hear we did not complete the mission and they hurt General Johnson."

Isaac grimaced. "Mateo and Andrea got away."

The Colonel chuckled. "Well, they made a mistake."

Isaac's face filled with confusion. "What was that?"

Brian pointed behind him. "They didn't kill him."

Isaac pushed past the doctors and scanned the bed. There lay the General with a silver cybernetic left leg and left arm. Blue lights ran down the side of both.

He peered at Mr. White. "Are these cybernetics to keep him alive?"

Mr. White examined General Johnson. "No. When she threw the rocket at him, he almost perished. When they found him, he was barely breathing, and missing two limbs. He asked for these enhancements to finish the mission."

Colonel Brian laughed. "Andrea made him mad. She shouldn't have done that."

Mr. White grinned. "Please excuse me, I have an urgent matter to oversee."

Brian and Isaac saluted. Mr. White returned to his office.

His aide stared at him. "She's waiting for you."

Mr. White stepped in and closed the door. An elegant African American woman in her early sixties stood before him via HoloConference. She stood five feet two inches tall, with chestnut brown skin, shoulder length black hair, and brown eyes. The woman wore a red dress with a pearl necklace and matching earrings.

She smirked. "You shouldn't keep me waiting."

Mr. White lifted his arm. "My apologies. I had to speak with our latest recruit and check the status of some special projects. We completed one, the other is almost done."

She smiled. "That sounds good. What do you need of me?"

Mr. White beamed. "Here's what I want you to do Mary."

She laughed. "Don't you mean Madam President?"

***

Liam parked the HoverVan in front of a single-story log cabin deep in the woods. The moon shined through the bare branches that surrounded it.

James looked at him. "Where are we?"

Liam turned off the van. "The family cabin my grandpa built."

James slapped his shoulder. "Is there a chainsaw, or a giant knife in there you wanna confess to having right now?"

Liam tried to grin. "Only if you make me mad."

The morose mood infected the vehicle.

They got out and Liam showed them a barrel. "Stick your suits in there. We'll grab fresh clothes in the cabin afterwards."

They removed their helmets and bodysuits and threw them in the drum.

Everyone had on shorts, undershirts, and shoes.

Liam placed an N950 mask on his face, poured lighter fluid on top of the gear, and set it on fire. They stepped up the stairs and moved indoors. Liam hit the lights.

The interior was immaculate. Light wood flooring contrasted the dark wood log walls.

It had a living room with a blue couch, coffee table, and a fireplace.

There was also a kitchen, two bedrooms, and a bathroom.

Liam handed out clothes that were left there. He worked on the fire while the others showered and dressed. Once the flames were going, he did the same. Liam joined them in the den. James, Robert, and Sofia sat on the sofa. Liam plopped down on the love seat.

James wore a blue shirt, a black jacket with a thick cotton collar, and blue jeans. Robert sported a black shirt, a charcoal jacket with scarlet mandarin letters on the rear, and black jeans.

Sofia had on a sunset gold shirt, a pair of his late mother's white jeans, and a brown hooded leather jacket.

Liam donned gray jeans, a red shirt, and a chocolate leather with an upturned neckline.

James clapped. "Let's figure out our next steps. Sofia, where do you think your mom and dad are heading?"

She shook her head. "I'm not sure. There are several places they might try."

James glanced at Liam. "How would we find them?"

Liam positioned his finger in the back of his ear. "Follow the sound of carnage after we rest. We need that to be at our finest."

The group agreed.

Robert smiled at his dad. "So, are you gonna do it?"

James shook his head. "I haven't decided."

Liam shrugged. "It may give us the advantage we need. How else could we prevent them from killing, or turning the entire world into Taken?"

James folded his fingers behind his neck and reclined. "It might kill us. We can't tell what might happen. If I die, who's gonna protect him?"

Robert peered at his father. "I think you should do it. It could give you a better chance to beat them. How will you keep me safe if they mutate everyone on Earth, and you're just human?"

Liam patted James' back. "I'll drink first. If it kills me, you're getting haunted for fun."

Sofia eyed them. "I'm confused. What are you talking about?"

James pulled out three vials of the Evolution formula from his pocket and placed them on the table. "I figured these are better away from your parents, and Mr. White."

Sofia's jaw fell.

Liam waved at her. "What do you think? We're two to one so far in favor of taking them. Your vote could force a majority or a stalemate."

He narrowed his eyes at her. "Do not cause a stalemate."

James stared at Sofia. "This is dangerous. We do not know how this will alter us. What if we become like your mother, turn into Taken, or die?"

Sofia smiled at him. "We almost died today. It's possible we will pass away tomorrow, next week, or the following month. Death is a part of life. My parents said we'd perish soon."

She grabbed James' hand. "My mom and dad are two of the greatest scientists on Earth. If they created this compound so Mr. White could have super agents, taking this may be the best chance we have at stopping them. Let's risk it to save the world."

Liam applauded. "Alright, majority rules."

They stood, picked up the vials, and exchanged a look. Liam consumed it first. James, Sofia, and Robert inspected him.

Liam stuck his tongue out. "It tastes worse than cough medicine."

After about a minute, Sofia drank her vial.

She closed her eyes, raised her hands, and shook them. "It's true. That is foul."

Sixty more seconds later, James emptied his container.

He scrunched his face. "Why isn't this flavored?"

Robert examined them. "Do you guys feel any different?"

They watched each other.

Liam rubbed his head. "Not really. How about y…"

He doubled over in pain. James reached out. "Hey, what's wrong?"

Liam fell and passed out.

James peered at Robert. "Help me move him to the couch."

After they moved him, Sofia contorted in agony and slumped forward. "It hurts!"

James caught her as she fainted. "Sofia, what's happening?!"

He lifted her and laid her on the loveseat.

James stared at his son. "If I pass out, grab a knife from the kitchen and protect yourself from any threat. Even m…"

He collapsed to his knees.

Robert rushed to him. "Dad!"

James fell backwards on the floor. He gazed at his child. *'What have I done?'* he thought.

Robert shook him. "Dad? Dad!"

Then everything faded to black.

TO BE CONTINUED

Acknowledgements

Book two, The Evolution, and book three, The Aftermath, are going through final edits and will release in 2024!

Special thanks to the following people: Tina, Miyah, Sammy, Mom, Noelle, Zuri, Chersti, ZeppelinDG, Sandy, Drew, Maddi, Rod, Phil, Kim, Jocelyn, Justin, Lindsey, Rue, Marsha, Dawn, Deb, David, Precious, Daniel, Jeremy, Lamont, Dianne, Donald, Shawndre, Wendy and Jason.